Y0-GDY-857

DUTY

DUTY

a novel

Jim R. Lane

Bridge Works Publishing Company
Bridgehampton, New York

Copyright © 1999 by Jim R. Lane

All rights reserved under International and Pan-American Copyright Conventions. No part of this book may be reproduced in any form or by any electronic or mechanical means, including information storage and retrieval systems, without permission in writing from the publisher, except by a reviewer who may quote brief passages in a review.

Published in the United States by Bridge Works Publishing Company, Bridgehampton, New York.
Distributed in the United States by National Book Network, Lanham, Maryland.

First Edition

The characters and events in this book are fictitious. Any similarity to actual persons, living or dead, is coincidental and not intended by the author.

Library of Congress Cataloguing-in-Publication Data

Lane, Jim R.
Duty : a novel / Jim R. Lane. — 1st ed.
p. cm.
ISBN 1-882593-29-4 (alk. paper)
I. Title.
PS3562.A484415D88 1999
813'.54 — dc 21

99-18832
CIP

To my wife,
Pamela,
for her love, strength,
encouragement and forbearance.

My deepest gratitude to Wendy Dager — literary agent, colleague, writer and friend; to Jacquelyn Powers for advice, counsel and gentle nagging; and to Alexandra Shelley and Barbara Phillips for their sharp editorial eyes.

When a stupid man is doing something he is ashamed of, he always declares that it is his duty.

— *George Bernard Shaw*

DUTY

✯ Chapter One ✯

Lieutenant Mark Palmer allowed himself this one bit of baiting — playing dumb while the CO of the USS *Modoc* waited for him to ask the obvious question — even at the risk of irritating his commanding officer. The skipper held a manila envelope near his face, as if inviting comparison to his own skin tone. The envelope wins, Mark thought. Mark pushed a lock of straight brown hair off his forehead and leaned forward, expectation shining in his hazel eyes. The captain's expression faded, along with any hint of theatrical tension.

"Well, it's a letter," the captain said.

Mark tightened the jaw muscles of his lightly tanned face and drew down the corners of his mouth to strangle a smile. His ears popped.

"And not just any old letter," the captain continued, attempting to save the moment. "I want you to read it. Carefully. You'll be action officer on this, Mark." Commander Morgan Baxter Bennett III leaned back and waved a match over a briar from the rack on his cluttered desk.

Mark stepped forward to receive the letter, then settled back in the metal chair and regarded Bennett. He and the skipper were the same height, about six feet, but the skipper was much heavier, at least thirty pounds. He carried his excess poundage strangely, all over his body. Someone in the wardroom suggested he had been inflated with a couple of pounds of air like a Macy's Thanksgiving Parade balloon. Mark mentally added that the air must be hot.

The envelope had "CO" on the outside in black ink — delivered directly to the commanding officer, skipping the chain of command. Mark examined it briefly while Bennett watched, nodding slightly in rhythm with the gentle rocking of his stuffed vinyl chair, turning slightly to gaze at the Navy base and bits of San Diego visible beyond. The captain's over-furnished cabin contained the single porthole below the level of the fleet tug's navigation bridge. Small, regular puffs of cherry blend smoke issued from Bennett's pipe, slowly filling the cabin as he made little humming noises into the briar's stem. Mark drew the several pages of lined paper from the envelope. The hand looked infantile in its mixture of block printing and cursive, and its oddly formed characters. In spite of the lines, the words drooped near the right edge as if they had melted. He flattened the crinkled sheets against his knee and read:

Dear Captain,

I know this letter aint coming threw the chain of command like I know letters are supposed to come and I hope you understand why I'm doing it this way and won't get too mad. I am writing to you because I cant keep this to myself no longer.

Anyways I reported aboard about three months ago and got assigned in A and E Division in engineering. Everybody was real nice to me and I didn't have no complaints. Petty Officer Lamm, my division leading petty officer, invited me over to his place for a steak dinner. Sort of a welcome aboard thing he says he does for all the new men in the division so I didn't think anything about it. We went to his apartment in National City and he cooked some steaks and we had some beer and tekilla and watched television for a while and then he asked me if I wanted to watch a porno flick. I said sure because I aint seen to many of them and he put it on his video player. We watched for about an hour until it got too boring. It wasn't a very good movie. Anyways, he took a shower and then I took a shower. He asked me if I wanted to sleep in the big bed with him and I said no I would be OK on the couch in the living room. He gave me a sheet and blanket and said goodnight. The next thing I know I woke up with a hard on and I felt something tugging on my gentiles. I looked up and saw Petty Officer Lamm on his knees by the couch playing with me.

I know this is wrong. I told him to quit and he didn't say nothing for a while just kept holding on to me. Then he went back to his bedroom. I tried to just forget about it but I cant. I cant look at Lamm no more and Chief Vega has chewed me out a couple of times for having my head up my ass. I am scared, sir, what is going to happen because I cant think about work when Lamm is around.

This is the truth. I am a Christian.

Very respectfully sir,
Randy Overmiller
Fireman Apprentice

Mark blew out a breath and leaned back. Shit, he thought, a queer case. Worst kind of mess in the Navy. Like a cancer. Catch one and he implicates ten others.

Chase them down. Investigate. Discharge them and hope to hell you get them all or it will only start over again — at least that's what they said in Military Justice School. He'd find out for himself now.

"Figured that would trip your trigger, Mark," the captain broke in on his thoughts. "How long will it take to get this Lamm character to court-martial?"

Mark sat straighter, surprised by the words. Court-martial. He'd never done one. He'd only been the ship's collateral duty legal officer for six months — one of the many jobs added on to his Administrative Officer assignment. "At this point, Skipper, I don't know if it's possible. There's not much here," he said, waving the letter gently, "Just some unsworn allegations. Even if they are true there probably wouldn't be enough evidence to stand up to a court-martial, probably not even to an honest captain's mast."

Mark had quickly become expert at preparing paperwork for captain's mast — nonjudicial punishment — the administrative forum where the captain could mete out punishment for minor offenses. In earlier times *justice at the mast* could have been whiplashes or keelhauling. "I'm assuming you want him out of the Navy if this turns out to be true. Can't do that with a single captain's mast. You have to —"

"Mister Palmer!" the captain broke in, "I didn't ask for a string of equivocations." Bennett's face reddened. "I want to know how long it will take you to court-martial this queer. I'll not have a piece of slime like this preying on my new men — or any men for that matter. You read me, Mister Palmer?" When the captain reverted to calling his officers "mister" — a practice that had been officially discouraged since the '70s — it was a clear sign to remain small and quiet.

"Captain, all I'm saying is a court-martial could turn into a can of worms here. It's practically impossible to prove anything on the basis of this one letter. I don't know anything about either one of these men, but Lamm has a good chance of beating the homosexual harassment charge if this is all the evidence we have. Once he's cleared by court-martial you can't take any other action."

Bennett started carving fiercely at the bowl of his meerschaum after Mark spoke, as if by concentrating on the pipe he wouldn't have to consider the lieutenant's answer. Mark wondered why Bennett was so single-minded about a court-martial when he had nothing more than Overmiller's letter. Was it some kind of blind vendetta or was he simply a committed homophobe?

Silence pervaded the cabin, broken only by the scratching of the pipe tool and a faint clang of machinery below decks. Mark watched the captain for a few seconds, expecting him to speak. When he didn't, Mark surveyed the cabin. His gaze settled on the *I-love-me* wall containing framed certificates for nearly every Morgan Baxter Bennett III act during his Navy career — for everything, for nothing. Potted grape ivy and spider plants swung from the overhead on Tijuana macramé, and piles of *Navy Times* newspapers and military history books covered every horizontal surface. Looks like a jungle swap meet, he thought. Dangerous as hell in a rough sea — but *Modoc* seldom spent much time away from the pier these days. The sailors had taken to calling it Building 210 — for the hull number painted on the ship's side and its lack of motion — suggesting it had become a permanent feature of the Thirty-second Street Naval Base. On the desk, the single rose in its silver bud vase from Bennett's home garden was the sole bit of elegance in the cabin.

It became clear Bennett was not going to speak. "Sir,"

Mark said, "it's not easy to prosecute anymore, with Article 31 rights, *Tempia* — Navy's version of *Miranda* — and the speedy trial thing. A man is even entitled to two free Navy lawyers plus whoever he wants to bring in from the outside. Then the legal center will probably advise against putting the case on the docket if the judge thinks it won't stand up to trial. They'll say they don't have time for spurious cases and this is the kind they put in that category. These days they don't consider it criminal unless the media gets hold of it and forces them into a court-martial."

Bennett laid the pipe on the green blotter before him and spoke quietly, earnestly. "I consider it criminal, Mister Palmer, and I'll not allow it under my command. I want that man prosecuted, court-martialed. Out. I'll not suffer cocksuckers on my ship. Dismissed."

In the empty passageway Mark flailed his arms, screwed his face into a grotesque mockery of Commander Morgan Baxter Bennett, and mimed, "I'll not suffer cocksuckers on my ship!" The thought struck him, wonder if that means we'll never have women assigned?

★

Mark's black Corfams *thunged* lightly on the metal ladder halfway down until he could reach the overhead bar and swing the rest of the way to the 0–1 level where he and *Modoc*'s six other officers shared staterooms. A man with a paintbrush stiffened in the passageway, surprised at Mark's approach. He hid a cigarette behind his paint-spotted dungarees. Seeing him, Mark felt his anger flare like an ember given a shot of pure oxygen. His immediate urge was to slap the man but instead he stood before the sailor, sniffing pointedly at the paint fumes and tobacco smoke mingling in the stale air. The sailor returned a baleful look that Mark had accepted as the standard response to a confrontation with a senior.

"Seaman Arnold," he said in a controlled voice, "you working on fire or suffocation?" Without waiting for an answer, knowing he wouldn't get one, he said, "Get rid of the cigarette and open some doors to the weather decks. Then get outside for a few minutes, you're already pale as a maggot."

Arnold hesitated for a protracted moment before moving slowly to carry out Mark's orders. Mark crossed his arms and remained on the spot he had chosen, turning only slightly to encourage the young sailor's momentum and, with any luck, his embarrassment at being caught.

Caught — what Arnold must think. Mark couldn't understand the resentment his orders generated. What's the Navy coming to, he wondered. It was an increasingly familiar question during the past few years with downsizing, base closings and Reagan's six-hundred-ship Navy, now under Bush and Clinton cut to fewer than half. It added up to longer deployments for the carriers and their battle groups — and sailors cutting their careers short to make better money as civilians. Mark continued down the passageway, wishing the ship were at sea.

USS *Modoc,* an ATF-210, the only ship in its class, was larger than the old Apache Class fleet tugs at two hundred and thirty feet overall with a forty-foot beam. *Modoc*'s role in the Pacific Fleet was limited now to towing gunfire targets, moving disabled ships and providing support for salvage operations.

The endless maintenance necessary to keep *Modoc* operational went on constantly while she was tied to the pier. The old ship's aging and obsolete equipment forced her engineers to make jury-rigged repairs. Parts were hard to find and the Navy supply system showed only reluctant support for a ship that could show up on the decommissioning list any day.

★

He tapped on the door marked EXECUTIVE OFFICER.

"Yep?"

"XO, it's Mark."

"Come on in, hoss."

Frank Madera had a stateroom to himself, though it was much smaller than the captain's and held only the essentials — a bunk, a desk, and two chairs. His locker stood open, revealing a few khakis and one set of whites. Frank dropped his *Penthouse* on the desk and swung his chair to face Mark.

"Been 'spectin' you." Frank's affectation of country boy speech had initially been an irritation to Mark but now he found himself playing along.

"Yepper." He felt vaguely silly mouthing the word that he thought probably meant agreement. "What do you think, Frank? Like a vigilante meeting in there. He's out for blood. Court-martial."

"Mark, you know the skipper's got major career fear — even more than the rest of us. If he's ever gonna get that fourth gold stripe, he can't appear to be soft on gays. *Modoc* is already a handicap to his career. And be careful about bringing up 'don't ask, don't tell' in front of him; in this outfit homophobia is still a virtue."

"This letter's really pushed him over the edge," Mark said.

"Wouldn't sweat it too much, bubba. He just got the damned thing this mornin' slid under the door like a cold draft. He'll calm down soon enough."

"You know this could tear the ship apart. Saw it happen on a carrier once during a cruise. A couple guys got themselves caught in the library gear locker giving each other flute lessons."

"Meat flute!" Frank interjected.

"Yeah. Anyway, a rumor flashed around the ship they were part of a ring of queers and that they were talking, naming names to save their own skins. Had to be locked up for their own protection. Whole damned crew was on edge, afraid their buddies were part of it. They should have been scared more of being named, whether they were gay or not, than of being propositioned. Proof didn't matter. Like a goddamned massacre. They could have been reading names out of the phone book. Anything to take the heat off of themselves.

"We were on cruise to the Gulf, ready to kick ass on Saddam. Everyone was set to strangle an Iraqi when all this came down. Since we were at sea there was no way to hold a court-martial, so the two guys were shipped back to Norfolk and discharged. Most of the crew never found out what happened to them for sure. Anyway, by the time it was over everybody was scared shitless not knowing if they'd been named. Nobody gave a shit about Iraq. Ruined morale. I'm afraid that'll happen here."

"You work on the case and I'll take care of morale." Frank dropped his good ole boy accent. Morale. That was his job, but one he clearly resented. A job that forced him to take flak from above and below, mediating between the captain and the crew. A buffer, middleman for the skipper, passing along unpopular policy as though it were his own while Bennett passed out medals at morning quarters. As a result, the captain looked like Santa Claus while the executive officer took the flak.

"Look, XO," Mark retreated to the less familiar title, "I want to discuss it with you so I don't fall on my sword.

Or yours, for that matter. I want to be sure we're on the same track."

Frank leaned back. Whenever he slouched, which seemed to be always, his shoulders came nearly level with his ears and he took on the look of a vulture waiting for something to die. "Sorry, Mark. It's just not what I need three months before I retire. Thought I'd be able to sail through 'til August, readin' porn and jerkin' off at the moon." He looked even more gaunt than usual as he sucked in his cheeks and passed a hand through short-cropped blond hair. "Suppose we're stuck with it though."

"I'm going to have to tell Dave Brown. Lamm and Overmiller both work for him," Mark said, seeing any chance of confidentiality slip away. Who would he have to tell next?

"Guess you can't do anything else if you're going to keep peace with Dave." He sighed in recognition of the protocol that required keeping other officers informed about anything that had to do with their men. Necessary, but a pain in the butt.

"I'm worried there won't be enough evidence for a court-martial, but the old man acts like he won't accept anything less. He's really hot on this."

"So what are you going to do?" Frank asked. He seldom offered advice, preferring, he said, to encourage his officers to find their own way. Some wondered if he had any wisdom to share.

"Well, of course I'll investigate, but if that's a bust I really don't know. Maybe he *will* cool down in a few days."

The men sat silent for a few minutes. Frank thumbed his magazine, riffling the pages like a deck of cards, a clear sign he wanted to return to it.

Mark fixed his gaze on the *Penthouse* cover and ignored Frank's signal to leave. His mind latched onto an old resentment: commanding officers who assumed something could be done simply because they wanted it. He saw it as a shortsighted abuse of the nearly absolute power given to ship captains. It was also a convenient way to affix responsibility should they lose control in the stiff Navy environment. The order had been given. That coupled nicely with the way blame was traditionally handled in the Navy. An officer merely accepted it — and the consequences — stoically, without defense or comment. A sign of integrity — assuming responsibility for mistakes over which one had no control.

With imminent retirement, Frank could afford not to care about the Lamm case. Mark still had four years before he could even consider retiring — on half his basic pay after twenty years' service — though he'd stay thirty if he could. But first he had to advance to lieutenant commander — without this promotion he wouldn't be allowed to stay in long enough to retire. One sub-par fitness report from Bennett and he'd be on the street. Don't like this case, he thought, smells bad already.

"Buy you a coffee, XO?"

"Naw. Got some work to do." Frank smiled as Mark headed for the door.

He walked down the short passageway and took the ladder to the main deck wardroom below.

Diminishing demand for services often left *Modoc* tied snug against the pier. She was now the only auxiliary fleet tug on active rolls. The whole Apache Class had been decommissioned years before, turned over to the Military Sealift Command or to Third World nations.

Modoc. Not a career-enhancing assignment. Mark hoped this tour aboard the old bucket was not indicative of his chance of getting his own ship to command when the time came — if he was still in uniform, if he weren't caught up in some Pentagon downsizing move. The Navy used to be a career with some stability. Now it wasn't much different from civilian industry, except for the possibility of getting killed in a war nobody cared about.

Mark couldn't forget the way he had felt when he first saw his orders. Worse, when he learned he wouldn't be the chief engineer but the administrative, personnel, legal, and any-other-lousy-position officer on *Modoc*. Shitty little jobs officer. Every ship had an SLJO, but Mark thought he had escaped the job, having gained nearly ten years seniority as an engineering officer. After three months as *Modoc*'s SLJO, though, the hurt had nearly disappeared, surfacing only occasionally when he felt particularly depressed. The rest of the time he attacked the position with vigor. He knew it would sound too hokey spoken aloud, so he told himself silently each morning he would be the best SLJO he could. It was his job and he'd "turn to" on it. That's what an officer does.

He admitted that some of it had turned out to be fun, and his uniforms stayed a lot cleaner outside the engine rooms.

Still . . .

☆ CHAPTER TWO ☆

MARK KNEW that his life would be getting complicated with the minutia of military justice even before he looked up court-martial procedures — rules of evidence, protecting everybody's rights, search and seizure — all of it in addition to his normal duties. He'd have to dig up references, chapter and verse, to speak intelligently about it to Bennett — do lots of staff work to satisfy the skipper. It came close to a religion, this propensity for the officer corps to nitpick every word in a sentence, each consideration in a decision, every nuance of meaning in unshined brass. Mark had learned to deal with it, actually enjoyed the exercise from time to time, priding himself on adaptability. Not always right maybe, but adaptable. Still, he resented the amount of time it took to look up, verify, or otherwise certify whatever he told the captain. In this case he wouldn't trust his memory or the four-week school that had taught him how to be the ship's legal officer. He'd spend the time in the *Manual for Courts-Martial* and be sure.

☆

The admin/personnel/legal office on *Modoc* barely provided room for files, two desks, and a pair of outdated computers. Personnelman First Class Jim Casso and Yeoman Third Gil Huff crawled into their seats like pilots packing themselves into an F–14 fighter. Customers stood in the passageway leaning on the Dutch door counter to conduct business.

Mark, like most of the officers, did paperwork in his stateroom and faced the choice of constantly phoning his men to bring him this instruction or that reference, or of getting it himself. He made the two-deck trip most of the time, thankful for even the slight exercise climbing the ladders provided. He refused to be intimidated by wardroom suggestions that he was Casso's and Huff's messenger. He hadn't forgotten his own six years enlisted time. He remembered how officers could be a royal pain, demanding, unappreciative, unable to wait a second for anything. Well, to be fair, he conceded, not all officers were like that. Some tried, as he did, to remember that "enlisted" didn't necessarily equate with "subhuman."

As Casso reached for the *Manual for Courts-Martial* and the *Judge Advocate General Manual* in the rack over his desk, his chambray shirt pulled free of his dungarees. The career petty officer carried extra weight around his middle, but it in no way hampered his efficiency. He had saved Mark's reputation a number of times already. The personnelman knew the books, having studied them for seventeen years. He knew the yeoman's job as well, to the everlasting dismay of Huff, who would prefer to take the day off — every day.

"Got a case, Lieutenant?" Casso asked, clearly eager for anything to enliven office routine.

"Don't know yet. Say, do you have the number for the command assistance desk at the legal service center?"

"Yes, sir. Taped inside the front cover of the *MCM*,"

he said as he handed the *Manual for Courts-Martial* and the *JAG Manual* through the Dutch door.

Mark leaned closer to Casso and lowered his voice. "Ever do an admin discharge board?"

"Yes, sir. A screamin' pain in the ass."

"Thanks." Mark wasn't encouraged.

He left the office with an additional bundle of personnel records to review. A crew of ninety-five didn't sound like many until you had to check each record individually against the manning documents from Washington. Donkey work, something Huff could do, but Mark wanted to get a feeling for the whole crew, read the evaluations. He'd already been stung into starting a humanitarian transfer for a seaman who convinced Mark his indigent mother would perish if he weren't nearby to care for her. Mark listened to the story and began the paperwork so it would be ready when the promised verification letters from a doctor, minister, and social worker arrived.

The kid had pulled the humanitarian transfer scam on whoever took the time to listen. Casso had let his lieutenant waste time with the seaman, reserving comment until Mark raged out loud about being taken in. The petty officer listened, hands behind his back as he leaned against the bulkhead waiting for Mark to finish. Then he calmly offered to screen all such cases — save the lieutenant's valuable time. Mark couldn't help but graciously accept Casso's offer, as he reflected on his own frustration with do-gooder officers of years past.

Lamm's file was in the stack. Mark set it aside, not wanting to form any opinions about the man too soon. Instead, he opened the *Manual for Courts-Martial,* searching for a charge under the Uniform Code of Military Justice that might apply. There was always Article 134. With its sixty different specifications and language charging "service discrediting conduct," it could be twisted to apply to a number of nonspecific cases. Probably be tough to use 134 in a court-martial with lawyers, judges, rules of evidence, and reasonable doubt. All a captain needed at mast, really, was a *reasonable desire* to nail the sailor before him.

Mark had little firsthand knowledge of the Navy legal system before spending a month at the Military Justice School at Fleet Training Center to prepare for his assignment on *Modoc.* As the ship's legal officer, he took care of minor cases but could call on real lawyers if needed. He was not shocked at the attitude of the four Navy lawyers and one Marine lawyer from the Judge Advocate General's Office who taught at the school; he was beyond that, but he was surprised. To them, justice didn't seem to be a priority, only winning cases or quietly rolling over, giving up in a gentlemanly way if it seemed politically propitious.

He remembered thinking there was something wrong with a system that routinely put the new JAG officers — the least experienced lawyers — in as defense counsels, creating a lop-sided contest favoring the Navy. Once the lawyers gained experience and began winning cases they were transferred into prosecution to argue for the government.

From the beginning the instructors implied that should the system cause distress among those few lily-livered officers one always finds in an organization the size of the Navy, one need only remember that if the accused wasn't a dirtbag to begin with, he would never have come to notice. Besides, a man found innocent from time to time lends an air of legitimacy to the system. The student officers laughed, unwilling to confront their instructors.

"The appearance of justice is as important as justice

itself," a lieutenant commander said, delivering the line as though he had recently returned from Mount Sinai. "Most defendants, though they can demand a court-martial when they are accused, opt for an appearance before the captain and will keep their mouths shut afterward. Of course there's always that five percent . . ."

They laughed again. But that was the real reason they were there in that overheated classroom — for the five percent.

Mark realized he had been staring at a page, seeing nothing, while replaying the dogma of the legal system from school. It all seemed different now. A joke back then. Today, grim.

He made an appointment with the command legal assistance desk for the following morning and reported to the captain that he was pursuing the court-martial route.

Bennett smiled and scraped at his pipe while Mark spoke, then leaned back in the large swivel rocker and plunked his heels on the desk blotter.

"You're a good man, Mark," the captain said, locking him in a fatherly gaze. "But more important, you're a good officer. I appreciate your telling me straight from the shoulder what's on your mind, what you believe. After all, I have to trust you as my legal advisor . . ."

Mark smiled slightly, as was expected. The old man was jerking him off with his phony honest-and-forthright line. Bennett's version of reverse psychology — when you sense them starting to feel their oats, getting rebellious — tell them how great they are. The offending officer is supposed to stumble all over himself with appreciation for the personal attention. Opposition usually disappears. In Mark's case it went underground.

". . . when I was a young officer . . ."

Mark conceded the captain was older, forty-three,

and had been an officer longer than he. Bennett tended to equate rank with age and never seemed to understand that several of his junior officers, having served a number of years as enlisted, approached his own age.

"... told the admiral straight out and was later awarded with his personally signed letter of commendation ..."

Mark wondered which frame on the captain's I-love-me wall held the letter.

"... with the selection board meeting next year I'm sure you really want to shine."

Mark stiffened. The selection board for lieutenant commander. Bennett's unmistakable threat. No psychology there. A sledgehammer. A bad fitness report from Bennett and he would fail-select. Two fails and he would have to leave the Navy with seventeen or eighteen years, in his forties and looking for a new job. He had already spent close to twenty years in the Navy, but the four years taken out for college didn't count as active service.

"... good for your career to handle the court-martial with your usual alacrity."

"Aye aye, sir," he said, and turned to the door when Bennett finished.

"Oh, and Mark, while I'm thinking about it, my parking sign on the pier is missing again."

"I'll mention it to the bo'sun, sir." The parking sign reserving the captain's space on the pier was a source of constant grief to the ship's Boatswain, Chief Warrant Officer Homer Pitkin.

"Spend more fuckin' time on them signs than ..." Homer's exasperation with them was not lessened by his inability to finish his sentence.

★

Official quitting time in port was 1600, when the crewmembers stood down from the day's work. Three-quarters of the sailors were then free to leave the ship. *Modoc*'s four-section watch bill meant twenty-five percent of the crew would be aboard at any given time to stand engineering, security and communications watches. Presumably, a single duty section would be able to get the ship ready to sail — or to actually get underway — in an emergency. An unexpected violent storm could batter an in-port ship against the pier. Chances to avoid loss or damage were better in the open sea — that took alert, available manpower.

Officers not on duty were expected to stay on board at least another half-hour past quitting time to set an example of dedication. Mark reluctantly went along with the game, compensating for the needless extra half-hour in other ways, allowing himself two fifteen-minute periods in his bunk — a tiny rebellion twice each day. Good for mental health. He loved the Navy — it was his home. Just the silly crap he couldn't stand.

At the stroke of one bell, 1630, he stepped onto the quarterdeck, saluted the first class petty officer standing Officer of the Day watch. "I am leaving the ship, sir."

The petty officer would be, in effect, in charge of the ship for four hours — the commanding officer's representative. As such, he returned Mark's salute. "Have a good evening, sir," he said as Mark stepped to the brow, turned to the fantail, and saluted the national ensign. The OOD saluted along with him. Ritual complete, Mark walked the short gangway to the pier, feeling the weight of the day slip away.

Mark had never grown tired of San Diego and treasured the sudden and often dramatic view of the city as he emerged from the ship's grim interior. He could make out the green patch of Balboa Park and in the opposite direction the red conical spires of the Hotel Del Coronado. The bay's jutting arm protected its waters from ocean swells, but winds across the low peninsula and the hot Santa Anas blowing out of the interior deserts made it prime territory for sailboats.

Lynn would be fixing gazpacho and cold poached salmon. Maybe some melon slices. He looked forward to dinner at her place. His own repertoire leaned heavily toward chili con carne, lasagna, or anything that would stand up to a merciless barbecue. He often thought of an old Jim Croce song to describe their different styles in more than cooking. "Salon and Saloon." He was never sure what Lynn saw in him but he refused to suffer the question for long. She had divorced Captain Tony Gianelli two years earlier for, as she put it, "chasing cunt all over the Orient and not having the decency to be discreet." It was the single vulgarity she allowed herself and she cherished it, waited to slip it into a conversation with Tony, she said — her rebellion against a lousy marriage and a good, Chicago North Side upbringing.

Lynn lived with her six-year-old daughter, Vicky, in an apartment in Chula Vista a short hop north of the Mexican border.

She met him at the door smelling of Shalimar and gazpacho, holding a wooden spoon as if she were a figure on a German clock ready to strike the hour of five on his head. Since the divorce she had taken to full denim skirts and tank tops sans bra. It always amused him the way her nipples came alive to greet him, standing at attention, begging for attention.

He scanned the room. All clear. The sound of a child's

tinny phonograph drifted from the bedroom. He cupped a breast in each hand and rolled each nipple between thumb and index finger while he kissed her, finding her tongue and a half-dissolved mint. He hooked the mint with his tongue and sloppily stole it from her mouth. They laughed while he wiped both their mouths with his handkerchief.

"Mark, Mark!" Vicky thundered down the hall, her tiny feet transmitting her entire forty-five pounds into bowling ball thuds on the floor. She ran with her arms out, bagging along in oversize Oshkosh overalls.

He scooped her high in the air, swung her in an arc around the living room twice, plunked her down on the floor, then dropped to one knee for her hello kiss and bear hug.

"Hiya, Vicky. How's my girl? How's school today?"

"Oh, all right, I guess." Her lower lip came out like a dresser drawer.

"She got in trouble," Lynn said.

"Must be tough, Vicky, can't even get away from Mom by going to school. What did you do?"

"She said a naughty word." Lynn stood above the two of them, arms crossed, red liquid dripping down the handle of her spoon into a puddle on her thumb.

"Oh? What word?"

"Mark! Don't encourage her to say what she was punished for. Vicky, don't you have numbers to work on?"

The little girl broke Mark's grip and ran back to her room.

"Sorry," Mark said, standing, "I still don't have a clue how to handle kids. Thought it was supposed to be instinctual. Good thing Cora and I didn't have any. Hell, we couldn't figure out how to handle each other."

Lynn walked back to the kitchen, poured a glass of Chardonnay for him, and passed it over the breakfast nook — peace offering — while he dragged a stool from under the counter.

"I shouldn't have snapped at you. Don't worry, you'll learn, and Vicky adores you."

"I ought to get her that aquarium we talked about. She'd have the fish to take care of. Fish I understand. Too bad you can't have a dog or cat here. Maybe if I was around more . . ." He caught himself. A subject that had been thoroughly wrung out.

"Maybe when I get my finances straight . . ." Lynn trailed off.

Lynn worked as a teacher's aide at the private school Vicky attended. Tony was obligated to pay Lynn's support for another two years. Then it would drop to child support money only. She wasn't ready to marry again though Mark was willing, and she feared if he moved in, Tony would sue to reduce his separate maintenance obligation. So Mark kept his own apartment while sleeping most nights at Lynn's, sneaking out early each morning before Vicky woke.

He moved to Lynn and put his hand on her shoulder. She turned, and he could see the tiny scar below her left ear — souvenir of a riding accident in her childhood — but which she jokingly claimed to have gotten in a Chicago South Side bar fight. "I really don't like it any better than you, Mark, but can you be patient for me? I need you and Vicky needs a father. Tony pays fatherhood lip service. When he's not at sea, he's gone to Vegas or Hawaii." Her face softened. "He called today, at school! Can you believe the nerve of that slug? Said he is going to retire next year and is thinking of a joint custody arrangement." Tears formed at the corners of her eyes and he drew her close. "I can't let him do that. He's no good with her — Uncle Daddy, the candyman. Mark, I know he's just doing it to get to me."

He couldn't say anything, only hold her. A minute passed and they stood there while she cried. She gasped a couple of times and drew back, wiping her eyes on the handkerchief he slipped into her hand. "I got mascara on your uniform. I'm sorry."

"That's all right. I've worn this one ten days now, gonna wash it next week, anyway."

She laughed and some of the blue sparkle returned to her reddened eyes. She bent forward, giving him a quick kiss. "Mister Palmer!" She copied the inflection Commander Bennett used as she had learned it from Mark. "That borders on insubordination."

He reached for her nipple but held short, catching a glimpse of Oshkosh overalls in the corner of his eye.

"Why's Mommy crying?"

"Because tomorrow night you're having dinner at my place."

"Oooh, yucky."

"Come here, you rug rat," Mark growled and chased her into the living room, capturing the child and kissing her cheek. "Finish your numbers? Well, go do them before dinner and I'll read you a bedtime story."

She scampered off, giggling, rubbing the wet spot he left on her cheek,

"Well done, *Mister Palmer.*"

☆

Mark waited in bed while Lynn completed her bathroom ritual. She sure never refuses me, he thought, like Cora had with every phony excuse I'd ever heard, finally to stop all together. How did I ever get mixed up with that one? Her only joy was my nine-month cruises and allotment checks.

The knowledge that Cora couldn't be bothered with his attentions, even on the night of his return from cruise, had given him increased freedom to explore the erotic smorgasbord in the Orient. Yet, like the other married officers, Mark worked out his PCOD — pussy cut-off date — so that any disease he might have picked up could be cured before reaching home. Mark sampled, but with careful discrimination. The AIDS epidemic had cooled most officers' ardor in recent years.

He gently stroked his penis to hardness as he relived a scene with a Eurasian woman in Singapore, seeing himself and that almond-eyed girl in the candle flame flickering on the table next to Lynn's bed. The woman had bathed him and herself, rubbed scented oil on their bodies until they glistened, then began her slow exploration of every square inch of his body with her tongue.

"Starting without me?" Lynn asked, pointing to the lump under the blanket. She stood near the bed in a long flannel nightgown.

"Just thinking about you. Happens all the time." He opened his eyes wide. "Take that thing off and get in here with me, honey."

He rolled over and blew the flame from the candle. He cupped his hand around Lynn's breast and drew her close, dipping his tongue between her teeth. He slid his other hand down her belly through the kinky patch of hair. The soft folds of antiseptically clean skin parted before his finger and he began a gentle massage. His knee between hers parted her legs as he pushed his erection against her side. Lynn put one arm across his back and dragged her fingertips in circles on his shoulder.

Mark's Singapore memory disappeared in the passion of this moment.

✯ Chapter Three ✯

MARK DRESSED QUICKLY in the predawn darkness, then woke Lynn. She lazed a hand to his head and pressed him deeper into her flesh. They shared this morning ritual because she hesitated to kiss him with her just awakened, pasty mouth.

He didn't mind the leftover taste of last night. He reveled in all her smells now that they had had a chance to develop with sleep, to overcome her scrubbing and rinsing the night before. She said it must be his peasant upbringing, but she indulged his small perversion. Secretly, he hoped she really enjoyed it as much as he did, sniffing and snorting, trailing his nose along her skin like a bloodhound on scent.

Outside, it was already light at five-fifteen. Not really sunup, he thought as he surveyed the sky. Wouldn't see the sun until late morning with the early overcast that lay like a heavy, wet wool blanket over San Diego. The rest of the day would be hot, uncomfortable in the confines of the ship.

He put his Fiat Spyder into first and idled into the street, coaxing it along with a light foot on the clutch. Lynn had asked him to get the muffler fixed but he protested the old one had been perfectly good for ten years and he didn't see any reason to take a chance on another. He reminded her how they both loved the wracking echo the old sports car made when they passed through a tunnel or freeway underpass top down at sixty-five. But there *were* the neighbors.

He snapped the catches over the windshield and flipped the soft top back with one hand. The moist, heavy air swirled around him as he reached a safe distance from the apartment and accelerated up the Interstate 5 ramp. Already the traffic had begun building in both directions, the stream of "green cards" from Tijuana headed north to their jobs in Coronado or La Jolla, and the vanguard of industrial workers headed to the South Bay. He would have a chance to eat a leisurely breakfast in *Modoc*'s small wardroom and prepare for the day's work before muster. He preferred not to think about the other reason for leaving early — to avoid Vicky so she wouldn't mention to her father that Mark was sleeping over.

"Who knows what he'll do?" Lynn had said, first in anguish, then in anger when Mark complained. But he knew she was right. Tony seemed to take pleasure in being a bastard, twisting the knife whenever he could, using Vicky in subtle ways to get to Lynn. He made Mommy the bad guy. Mark urged Lynn to get tough, stand up to Tony. But as long as Tony had any financial control over her life, she balked. Mark offered her money if she didn't want marriage, help with support until she could work into a teaching position at school. *"And what do I do when you find someone else?"* she had said. Her mistrust of men had surfaced those few times when they had argued. Each time Mark had protested that he had no intention of finding someone else. Lynn would then calmly cite Tony who had left her and her father who had blamed his dalliances and eventual divorce from her mother on his own *mid-life crisis.* She reminded Mark that he had left Cora. *"Every man I know is a runaway."*

He had no answer.

★

At the Naval Legal Services Office, Mark asked to speak to someone about setting up a court-martial and was directed to the Command Services desk. Mark didn't mean to gape at the bizarre-looking JAG officer he approached, but could not tear his eyes away. Lieutenant Alvin Finney accentuated his sunburst face, beaky nose, and prematurely gray fuzz of hair with a pair of round, black-framed glasses. A cartoon owl, Mark thought.

Finney locked his magnified eyes on Mark's and grinned. "Can I offer you a cup of coffee, Lieutenant Palmer, or tea? Maybe a field mouse?" he said, reaching across the desk to clasp hands. Mark reddened, ashamed of his unabashed appraisal of the officer and having his mind so easily read. He quickly averted his eyes, surveying the pale green office with its haze-gray metal furniture — like a hundred other anonymous government offices.

"Not to worry, I only attack at night, and then mostly rodents." Finney chuckled. "I thought that looking wise would be an asset for a lawyer, that's why I studied my buns off to be one. Big mistake," he said. What can I do for you, Lieutenant . . . Mark?"

"My skipper found this under his door yesterday and wants a court-martial." He passed the Overmiller letter across the desk.

Finney appraised the envelope, turning it over in his hands then placing it on the desk blotter before patting the edges with his palms, gently nudging it straight and square on the desk as if it were a freshly shuffled deck. "Unless he assembled a crowd at high noon on the fantail and gave the captain a blow job, you're wasting time, pissing up a rope."

"How did you know?" Mark asked.

"Easy. What else could it be? Eighty-five percent of the homos get nailed by a buddy, a jealous lover, or someone who just has it in for them. The other fifteen percent either confess to get a quick discharge or are actually caught in the act." He grinned and his nose tipped down. "Can't tell you how many fakers who just want out actually consider sucking a dick before witnesses to convince the old man. But who knows, it might start a whole new way of life for them. That's what they are scared of — finding out they like it." He nodded to the letter. "I'd guess it is a junior accusing a senior man, right?"

"A fireman and a first class."

"Well, before you start building the gallows, take a look at what motives the fireman might have."

"Of course I'll investigate, but the captain is pretty adamant about it."

"Captains can get away with being adamant . . . to a point."

"What do you mean?"

"They can do pretty much what they want most of the time, but if they get too carried away there are review boards that can give these cases a close look. "

"He doesn't seem to be concerned about that."

"Okay, so your captain wants to hang the guilty bastard, make him walk the plank for an affliction, a perversion, a deviance that affects twenty percent of the male population of this country. That's what's criminal." He spoke in a firm but rising tone as if accusing Mark of owning the defective commanding officer.

"If we found and court-martialed every man and woman in the Navy who ever had a homosexual experience, half our ships would never get underway." Finney was on his feet. "I'll stake my next paycheck on this being an uncorroborated, vague, undated, incoherent plea for justice from a good Christian." To Mark's startled look he continued, "Yes, Lieutenant, they're all good Christians. Makes them think you'll believe the crap they write. Comes from the heart, you know, and it's a sin to tell a lie."

Mark could think of nothing to say.

Finney dropped into his chair, soliloquy complete. "Thank you for bearing up to my performance. I do it about every other week, whenever I get one of these." He held the envelope like a putrefied dead cat, dangling it from two fingers while he turned his head away from the imaginary stink, wrinkling his nose. He dropped it to the blotter and opened it.

Mark liked this owl-lawyer and his theatrical way of making a point. It was strange that Bennett had raised such a ruckus about the letter, preferring to believe Overmiller without so much as an investigation. Maybe the XO had a point about Bennett doing whatever it took for promotion.

While Finney read the letter Mark considered what the lawyer had said. Irrational fear did seem to be generated by the very mention of homosexuality aboard ship. The men were always playing grab-ass games and making lewd offers and suggestions to each other. But that was in the open, in the spirit of fun and camaraderie.

"Unless you can come up with more than this — like a complete confession from Lamm or some corroborating testimony *and* a sworn statement from Overmiller and a willingness to testify in court — you haven't got a chance. But supposing you did find enough to get as far as the courtroom on merits. It would still be tough to really nail this one down if Lamm fights it. He could get a civilian lawyer, play it up in the press like that Air Force officer a couple years ago. Or more recently, like the Navy chief petty officer who got caught when he posted a notice on the Internet looking to meet someone with a similar inclination. But that's all hypothetical and assumes Lamm is gay or would admit to it and fight to stay in the service," he said, waving his arms at the ceiling. "What you have here shouldn't stand up to a captain's mast."

"Kind of thought so. Tried to talk the captain out of pressing charges on the basis of this letter alone. If he calls your CO, will he get the same story you just gave me?"

"Sure. But I tell it better."

"Thanks." Mark went to the door. "Guess I'm stuck with an admin discharge board if I can't get more evidence."

"Right. That's the best way if your skipper pushes this. Here's a copy of the Secretary of the Navy's Instruction and the format book for the board. It should be all you need."

★

"Then get more evidence!" the captain thundered, as if Mark could go to a drawer marked EVIDENCE — REAL AND CIRCUMSTANTIAL, and pluck out what he needed for a conviction.

"I wanted you to know there may not be any more evidence. This letter might be a line of shit. Overmiller may have been put up to it, or may have some grudge to settle. I don't think we should automatically assume the allegations are true without investigating."

"Then investigate, *Mister.*"

"And if whatever I uncover is still short of what's

necessary to win in court, we're still in a bind. I want you to know, Skipper, that we may have to go the route of admin discharge. I mean, you want Lamm out? It can be done without the court-martial. And, really, the admin board is something we could conduct ourselves, right here. Gives us a certain amount of control. You can even disagree with the board's findings before their recommendation goes to the Bureau for final approval."

Bennett leaned back in the chair. He seemed momentarily calmer. Then he leaned forward after a few seconds and began rearranging desktop items — the stapler, the white marble and gold pen set, his pipe rack — with choppy movements. Mark had never seen him this way, this passionate, over anything. He wanted more than justice for the alleged harassment; he wanted revenge, it seemed, against Lamm for being a homosexual. Why not against Overmiller for bringing it up?

"How about getting Naval Investigative Service involved in this? Surely NIS is better prepared to find the evidence we need." Bennett clung to the court-martial.

The special agent Mark had phoned earlier dismissed his query as if he were being asked to take out the garbage. "I spoke to an agent about it. He said, 'NIS doesn't have the time or talent to chase queers.' Said they are up to their eyeballs in drug cases. He mentioned the ratio of convictions is disappointingly low. Got to concentrate on the high-yield cases."

Bennett looked away from Mark, who remained standing at parade rest before the desk, as if he were on trial. "So what are you trying to tell me, that we're stuck with this mess?"

"It seems the prevailing attitude is that we should handle this administratively, that taking a homosexual, even an admitted homosexual, to court-martial constitutes persecution rather than prosecution. Of course, when I investigate — still have to do that even for an admin — if something turns up that points to real criminal activity, I'll get NIS on it."

"All right, Mark. Go ahead, but I'll be watching this thing very closely. You know my desires here." Bennett lifted the yellow rose from the vase and sniffed it, dripping water from the stem onto his shirt. "Don't disappoint me." He dismissed Mark with a wave of his hand.

In the passageway Mark allowed his face to tighten into a scowl. That son of a bitch, he thought, acts like I'm the queer. *"Don't disappoint me."* What does he think I should do — shoot Lamm and deliver his head on a platter?

In his stateroom he called Petty Officer Casso. "Track down Fireman Overmiller for me, would you, and send him to my stateroom." He kept his voice light, just another piece of minor business to handle. He trusted Casso to keep his mouth shut but was aware how rumors started and spread. This would all come out in the open soon enough.

He dialed the engineering control room and waited while the watch found Lieutenant Brown. "Dave," he said to his roommate, "I wanted to let you know I sent for one of your men — Overmiller. Got to talk with him for a while. I'll fill you in on it later."

"Sure, Mark. No sweat. I'll pass it along to his division chief."

It didn't do a thing for secrecy to have to call Dave, who would tell his assistant to tell the division chief that the legal officer wanted to see Overmiller, but it was routine, a courtesy. Officers and chiefs could easily turn uncooperative if not consulted. You couldn't afford enemies aboard if you were to remain effective.

Mark slipped a "rights sheet" from his neat file drawer in the small secretary-style desk. He and Dave each had a desk in the confined space but when the writing surfaces of both were opened a chair wouldn't fit between them. Dave left the sleeping quarters to Mark to use as an office. As the ship's chief engineer, Dave had less paperwork. He used a table in the wardroom when he had to get away from the cramped engineering office and noisy machinery spaces. The arrangement suited Mark. The quiet stateroom on the 0–1 level was a good spot to interview or interrogate, depending on whether he happened to be wearing his admin or legal hat.

He had finished copying Overmiller's full name and social security number from the ship's roster onto the rights sheet when a timid knock sounded on the door. "Come in."

"You want to see me sir? I'm Overmiller." A small dungaree-clad man, a boy really, stepped cautiously into the room. He held the door ajar and left one foot in the passageway. His dark eyes were the most remarkable thing about him, liquid, but at the same time with the frightened wideness of a startled animal. His dark, almost black hair had a tousled look and was a bit longer than regulations could be stretched. Teenage acne had not quite finished with his face and neck, and a few hard, red bumps spotted his skin.

"Come in, Fireman Overmiller," Mark said in an even tone, remaining as emotionless as he could. "Have a seat." He motioned to a folding chair. He waited until the man was seated and had a look around the tiny room before he spoke again.

"I suppose you already figured out that I called you here to talk about the letter you sent to the captain concerning Petty Officer Lamm."

"Yes, sir, but I thought the captain would call me."

"I'm the legal officer and handle all these matters. Captain Bennett's too busy running the ship to handle every matter personally, so he spreads the responsibilities out." Mark stopped, surprised he was talking this way, as to a child. Overmiller knew damned well how the ship was organized. "He's seen your letter, rest assured. I'm going to ask you some questions about that letter and what happened at Lamm's place, but before I do, I want you to go over this rights sheet with me." He picked up the paper.

"Rights?" A shadow of fear crossed his face. "I didn't do anything wrong."

"Well, suppose Petty Officer Lamm accuses you of something. Just suppose. What you tell me here today could not be used in the proceeding as documentary evidence if you weren't informed of your rights before talking to me. If you tell me the truth, the rights sheet is just so much paper. Understand?"

"I think so."

Mark hoped to make Overmiller think seriously about whatever he planned to say. He wanted the accuser to bear responsibility for his own words. If it turned out to be a lie, the rights sheet and sworn statement would be prima facie evidence of a violation of Article 107 of the Uniform Code of Military Justice. Not entrapment. Insurance. They'd taught him well at Justice School. Besides, if the Lamm thing fell through, he could offer the captain an airtight case against Overmiller.

Cover your ass, Lieutenant, he said to himself, handing Overmiller a pen. "Initial in the margin if you understand the rights as I read them aloud. If you don't understand, ask and I'll explain further. 'I have the right to remain silent.' Understand?"

He finished the list of rights and went to the section that waived the rights. Overmiller's hand became less steady as he moved down the sheet, his initials covering progressively more area.

Mark reached the last line and read the item aloud in the same matter-of-fact voice. " 'This acknowledgment and waiver of rights is made freely and voluntarily by me and without any promises or threats having been made to me.' Go ahead and initial that if you understand and sign below."

He placed the completed sheet in a drawer, his ace in the hole. He wasn't about to let this little creep screw up his chance of making lieutenant commander.

"Now tell me what you can." He snapped on the small cassette recorder on the desk and turned the microphone toward Overmiller.

✮ Chapter Four ✮

Lieutenant Will Tapia, the operations officer, sat near the end of a long table in *Modoc*'s officers' wardroom, chiding the supply officer, Lieutenant junior grade Bert Kastner, about an overdue order of navigation plotting sheets. The "pork chop" — so-called for the shape of his Supply Corps collar insignia — shrugged, raising his palms in a gesture of helplessness, promising he would pass Will's displeasure along to the supply center. Standard banter, though both knew Bert was a whiz at his job, particularly in the face of dwindling resources. Part of it was taking good-natured ribbing. The talk was loud enough to cover Mark's explanation to Dave Brown as they faced each other at the small table in the wardroom corner.

The engineer looked hurt, as though he was the one accused wrongly. His mood changed quickly to hostility. "I can't afford to lose anyone now, especially a petty officer who runs a whole goddamned division by himself. I'm already undermanned."

"I sympathize, Dave, but the old man is hot on this. Already threatened me with a fitness report that would shitcan my career. I just wanted to let you know what was going on before you figured it out yourself and came down on my case. Maybe we can work together on this, keep the turmoil in your department to a minimum. All right?"

"What you say, I don't have much choice, now do I?" Dave let the sarcasm flow before taking a bite from one of the bean and cheese sandwiches on his plate. He tossed the sandwich down and leaned back in the chair. "Sorry, Mark. This is all so preposterous. If you knew Lamm you could see it. He's not only good; he's the most even-tempered sailor I know."

"It's all right. I'd be pissed, too."

Dave Brown was in a clean uniform, even though his job kept him constantly dirty. Bennett's rule — changing to dine twice a day then back into filthy coveralls — usually put him in a foul humor during meals.

"How bad does it look, Mark?" Dave lifted his sandwich.

"Bad enough. Overmiller was shaky but he stuck to his story. I warned him to keep quiet about this or I'd have him up on an orders violation. It's going to get around eventually, though. These things always do. I'm going to interview Lamm this afternoon. That will tell us a lot — I hope. I'll ask him for a consent search of his apartment, so he may be away for a while. What else can you tell me about him?"

"Shit-hot petty officer. Can't figure out why he hasn't made chief yet. Got a degree from UCLA and is working on his master's. Economics or English, don't remember which."

"Are you serious? What's he doing an enlisted man?" Mark registered his surprise.

"Says he likes it. Runs A and E Division by himself under Chief Vega. His men like him and bust ass to please him. Except for this turd Overmiller who's been a pain in the butt since he's been here. He can be entertaining sometimes, but I need workers, not comedians. Never passes inspection at quarters. They find him sleeping under a workbench when he's supposed to be on evaporator watch." Dave dragged his oversized spoon through the film forming on the beef barley soup that had chilled in the bowl. "I guess that's what pisses me off so much about this. Some dirtbag makes an accusation and my best man goes through the wringer. Was going to put him in for Limited Duty Officer this year. Make a hell of a fine mustang officer. Can't do a thing while he's under suspicion. Skipper'd have to sign off on it."

"I'll try to wrap it up as fast as I can, Dave, but unless Overmiller can be proven a liar pretty quick, it could take some time. Even if it doesn't go to a court-martial, if there's enough evidence we'll have to do an admin board."

The two sat silently, poking at the plates before them. Ensign Gordon Mackey, Dave's assistant, came in and took a seat beside him.

"You sure know how to fuck up lunch," Dave said softly, keeping his eyes on the table.

Mackey looked hurt. "Sorry, boss," he said as a mess cook plunked a ration before him, "What'd I do now?"

The two older men chuckled at the ensign's immediate acceptance of blame and went back to their lunch while Mackey sat openmouthed, his own soup chilling rapidly.

★

"Come in, Petty Officer Lamm," Mark responded to the knock. He checked his watch — 1400 — exactly on time.

The slender, well-tanned sailor stepped into the

stateroom and stood easily near the door, glancing briefly with gentle brown eyes at the lieutenant's spartan accommodations. Mark sized him up quickly. About six-two — he'd have to be careful moving in the ship's confined spaces. Like all tall men aboard ship, Lamm maintained a slightly stooped posture — a matter of skull survival under the restricted overheads. He'd seen Lamm around the ship, but had taken no particular notice. Now, up close, he understood why Dave was so upset at the thought of losing him. The good men stood out. Not unlike myself, Mark thought, without a trace of embarrassment. It was what had gotten him four years of Navy-paid college and a commission. Lamm had that same quality, attention to detail. He would never be caught in ragged dungarees. They'd be soiled and stained from the job possibly, but the shirttail would be tucked, the gig line perfect, belt buckle regulation and gleaming. The similarities between Mark's and Lamm's appearances were striking and troublesome.

Lamm kept his sandy hair severely short on the sides. On him it didn't look like a scalping. An example for the men to follow. The dungaree shirt bore a neat stencil over the left pocket, his last name bisected by a knifelike crease. Another ran through the right pocket. Without seeing his back, Mark knew there would be three vertical creases in the shirt placed precisely equidistant.

"Please have a seat," Mark said, feeling increasingly uneasy, almost as if he were the accused. He had gone over Lamm's record following lunch and found, if anything, Dave had been too modest in his praise of the man.

"I don't know any other way to say this, Petty Officer Lamm, so I'll just come out with it. You have been accused of making homosexual advances to one of the men on the ship."

Lamm's face showed no emotion. Mark expected none with the tip-off he had given — *no other way to say this* — a foreshadowing of bad news. The sailor had instinctively grasped the instant to steel his features, lash down his feelings until he got all the information, until he was alone with it. The good men knew how to suppress an explosion, accept any news with a straight face. But the man's brown eyes were two-way windows and Mark detected sudden fear in them as Lamm's gaze darted around the room, to the papers on the desk, finally settling on a spot on the bulkhead behind Mark.

It could mean anything. Fear of being exposed, or simply fear of being drawn into the military justice machine to be spit out the other end, innocent or guilty, but battered in either case.

"Who's accusing me, Lieutenant?" Lamm's question came out flat, toneless.

"I'm not going to mention any names right now. Got to get a few things sorted out first. With your consent, I would like to search your apartment."

"All right, sir," Lamm answered after an extended pause, "I suppose if I refuse that will be taken as an admission of guilt."

"Not at all," Mark said. "You are entitled to your privacy. Do you still consent?"

"Yes, sir."

"Don't say anything more to me about this case until I can give you your rights. First, though, we can get the search out of the way. You can take someone along as a witness."

"I'd like Chief Vega to go."

The dark, stocky chief arrived sweaty and irritated. A glance at Mark and Lamm and his expression changed to one of concern. He stepped close to Lamm's chair and put a hairy paw on his shoulder.

"Petty Officer Lamm has asked for you to be his witness during a search of his apartment, Chief. Are you willing?"

"Well, yes, sir. What's this all about, anyway?"

"Lamm has been accused of homosexuality," Mark answered as impersonally as he could.

"That's absolute bullshit. Sir," the chief responded, lifting his hand from Lamm's shoulder then pausing a moment, awareness in his eyes that he had for a split second believed the charge. He dropped his hand again to the blue chambray shirt, patting the shoulder, turning his flinch into a gesture of confidence. "Lamm here ain't no more queer than me."

"I hope that's what we find out. In the meantime, I've asked him not to talk to anyone about this until I can take his sworn statement, so please don't try to discuss it with him, Chief, and keep it to yourself. I want to avoid any further embarrassment."

"Yes *sir,*" Chief Vega answered, as if having just been given a life or death mission.

★

"Over to the desk, Lamm. Do a little paperwork here, keep this all legal and aboveboard." Naval Investigative Service Agent Berquist kept an even tone that belied an undercurrent of suspicion evident in his eyes and movements. He never turned his back to Lamm and occasionally touched the snub-nosed pistol he kept in an open frame holster in the small of his back. The *Modoc* group had stopped at the NIS office to meet up with Agent

Berquist, who had reluctantly agreed to supervise the search of Lamm's National City apartment.

National City, wedged between San Diego and Chula Vista like a vagrant among opera goers, fronted the Naval Base but somehow avoided the title "Navy town" reserved for San Diego to the north. Little doubt existed among the National City locals and the sailors that it was just that. The town had a perpetually dull look, as if it had just weathered a dust storm. Men from the ships could walk out the Eighth Street gate and in a few blocks find fast-talking used car dealers who catered to the inexperienced; a triple-X porno theater — long since converted to a cheap furniture store with the advent of videotaped pornography; and a tattoo parlor catering, increasingly, to high schoolers wanting body piercing. A man could dine on pizza or Filipino or Mexican food while waiting for something wonderful to happen. Or he could make it happen in a *WestPac widow bar* where wives of Navymen who were deployed on ships in the western Pacific gathered — when they could find a babysitter.

Lamm's apartment was the second floor of a stuccoed 1920s shamble with an outside stairway. It needed paint, but the small yard below was well-kept. Vegetables grew in a carefully tended plot a foot-and-a-half wide and twenty feet long bordering one of the two narrow tire strips of concrete that led to the separate, single-car garage. The apartment entrance was through a small service porch, lined with crude shelves of canned goods covered with plastic gingham curtains. The four men — the NIS agent, Mark, Lamm and Vega — moved slowly, shuffling in small steps as if in a museum. They stared at the accouterments of existence as though they might contain some clue to the sexuality of the owner.

The kitchen appeared to be efficient and the window

over the sink offered a pleasant treetop view of the neighborhood. On the table, the soggy remains of a quick breakfast of Cocoa Puffs lay in a plastic bowl, with a half-finished cup of coffee beside it.

Reacting to a sound from the living room, Agent Berquist drew his gun from the flat holster at his back and dropped to a crouch. He moved slowly to the door, motioning the others to stay back. The pistol clamped in both his hands practically disappeared. Only the ugly, fat barrel poked beyond his thick fingers. He darted a look around the doorsill, then moved quickly into firing position, holding the impressive pose for a second before standing upright and reholstering. Berquist stepped boldly into the room.

Mark moved forward and saw that the agent was ready to defend them from a man lying on the couch under a sheet tented with his erection.

A toilet flushed and another man wearing only blue bikini briefs stepped into the room scratching his long matted hair, rubbing his eyes. He stopped, startled by the roomful of invading men.

He looked at Lamm, a question painted across his face. "Thought the party was over," he said, and walked into the bedroom.

☆ Chapter Five ☆

BERQUIST BENT TO THE TASK of showing his expertise: probing dirty laundry, checking the undersides of drawers as if he expected to find a stash of cocaine, maybe some secret microfilm. The absurdity of the search struck Mark as he halfheartedly poked through a stack of videocassettes. What were they looking for? What were the signs a homosexual lived here? The two men? Could say the same about rooms in the Navy barracks.

He found the tape Overmiller had mentioned in his statement, *Lunchtime Lust*. The label showed a photograph of two women and a man sprawled across a desk, wearing expressions of exquisite carnal joy, tongues thrust out, eyes closed.

Lamm sat in an armchair, staring at his knees, rubbing his temples slowly with stiffened fingers. The search had been underway for several minutes when the man on the couch woke with a start and drew the sheet up to his neck, watching warily as the men moved around the room. The man in blue skivvies came from the bedroom wearing gray sweat pants, and plunked down on the couch, pushing the other man's feet aside.

Everyone except Berquist was obviously embarrassed and avoided eye contact. The agent merrily pawed his way through the living room to the bedroom, leaving a mess in his wake. Mark followed, straightening books and knickknacks left askew, closing drawers.

The agent called Mark and Chief Vega into the bedroom.

"Lookee here," Berquist exclaimed, holding the closet door wide as if he were about to usher in a celebrity. They moved forward to peer into the small cubicle lit from above by a dangling bare bulb. "What do you see?" He tested them.

"Shoes, clothes, fishing pole," Mark offered, puzzled at what he was missing in the absolutely conventional closet.

"Not just clothes," Berquist said, lowering his voice to little more than a whisper. "Uniforms." He plucked a black sleeve from the rest and gestured to the security force patch sewn to it. "Rent-a-cop. Here's a gas station uniform." He dug the short sleeve out. "And this looks like one of those, whatchacall 'em, drive-in restaurant uniforms."

"McDonald's," Chief Vega offered.

"Is this important?" Mark asked.

"Yer lookin' for queers? Well, homos like to dress up in uniforms when they go out. Sort of a sign to others that they're available. Like women used to put a rose behind the right or left ear to let guys know if they were married or wanted to fool around, like."

Mark stared at the agent, realizing he knew nothing about the gay lifestyle other than the obvious. He supposed it would be handy to have some method to identify homosexuals among themselves, but this seemed a strange way to do it. How many thousands of people wore uniforms at work? he thought, realizing that he had khakis on at the moment. "A lot of people wear uniforms, Mister Berquist," Mark said, indicating his own and Chief Vega's clothing.

"But do you go to gay bars in uniform?" came the answer, as if that settled the issue.

Mark was unsure how to answer Berquist or even if there was an answer to his illogic. The wild jump from bedroom closet to a gay bar where uniforms were a sign of availability had taken him by surprise.

Berquist seemed not only pleased with his find but almost jovial as he pushed the hangers sideways to reveal the uniforms one by one. Mark started toward the living room when Berquist called to him.

"How 'bout sending the gold dust twins in here one at a time. I want to talk to them."

The two men on the couch were quietly talking when Mark interrupted to ask if they would speak with him or the agent. Maybe a statement would give him something to go on. He assumed they were not in the service from the length of their hair. With no jurisdiction over civilians off base, there was little he could do but ask.

Blue Skivvies shook his head, answering for them both. "This ain't anything to do with us. Why'n't you guys just get out. Everything's all right here — no bogey men." The second man leaned to the side, yawning, resting his head on the couch arm and remained silent.

Lamm still sat, fingers making small circular motions against his temples. Mark knew that everything definitely was *not* all right, that Lamm was at the top of a roller coaster ride that was going downhill in something close to free-fall.

Berquist came out of the bedroom, glaring at the two men on the couch, then took Mark by the arm and steered him into the kitchen. "You see any magazines in here anywhere?"

"Huh?"

"Magazines, magazines. You know, *Penthouse, Hustler.*"

"Uh, no."

"Aha!"

★

When Mark got home that evening, Lynn and Vicky had already arrived and let themselves in. Vicky was sprawled on the couch with her crayons, coloring an elephant orange. He kissed them both and hurried into the bedroom to change into Levi's and a T-shirt.

"Well, how did you save us from the threat of worldwide terrorism today?" Lynn asked. The question, almost a ritual with them, was her way of bringing him back to what she called "humanity." She had never been particularly impressed with the air of self-sacrifice many Navy men wore like the Medal of Honor. Whenever Mark complained, she would ask him why he had stayed in so long if it was so bad.

"You're going to love this one, Lynn," he said, accepting the glass of wine she offered. "Did a consent search of a sailor's apartment. Not one of my better days. Didn't save anyone."

"Still playing the game, though, aren't you?"

"What am I supposed to do? It's my job — paycheck, you know. Bennett already made his desires perfectly clear about this case. He's made it perfectly clear my next fitrep depends on it."

"I didn't think fitness reports bothered you."

"Never did because they've all been good. This one's important because the lieutenant commander selection board is coming up. Two bum fitreps and I can kiss that promotion good-bye and my career along with it."

"Can't you appeal somewhere to get it changed? People were always writing to Tony to fix fitreps he had written on them years before."

"You think Bennett would change one once he wrote it? Not much chance. That would be admitting fallibility. Besides, Navy's looking for ways to thin certain ranks these days. Just like corporations."

"So what are you going to do?"

"I won't give him a reason to write a bad report."

"It's all so childish and picky. How can you stand it?"

He shook his head and shrugged. "How about veal cordon bleu," he said, changing the subject, "tender slices of zucchini in a light egg batter, spinach salad, and chocolate mousse?"

"You have all that?"

"No, but I thought it would be nice to think about it. Barbecued hamburgers is what I have."

After dinner Vicky slept on the rug, the flickering glow of the television playing over her while Mark and Lynn, elbows propped on the kitchen table, sipped small glasses of brandy.

Mark told her about Lamm's case while she reacted with a mixture of interest and disgust.

"So what are you going to do about it?"

"Not sure. Berquist, after all that noise about uniforms, submitted a negative search report — didn't even mention the two guys! So I'm back to the letter and Overmiller's statement."

"Mark, I can't really see how it matters what these guys do in their own apartments. Why should you care, or anybody else?"

"Think of it this way. How would you like to have to

go to work someplace where the boss is constantly trying to get into your pants? You know if you don't give in, you'll get the worst jobs and lousy efficiency reports."

"Ha!" She thumped the table and they both instinctively glanced to see if the noise had wakened Vicky. "I knew it! It's all right for women to have to put up with that abuse for years, but soon as one of your precious sailors gets propositioned you go to battle stations."

"Huh?"

"Mark, don't you realize that you just described what's been happening to women as long as they've worked for men?"

He creased his forehead. "Never thought of it that way. But it's still wrong."

"Men are so dense sometimes. *Of course* it's not right. That's the whole point, nobody notices it's not right until it happens to a man."

"But I'm not sure it happened." He could see the conversation getting away from him.

"So what if it did? It's not the end of the world for Over — whatever his name is — if Lamm fed him and tried to cop a feel. You did the same thing to me on our first date."

"But it's against military law to make homosexual advances. It could ruin discipline on the ship."

"You believe that? How's discipline now?"

"Pretty good, actually, when you consider we're getting downsized out of existence."

"Then you're telling me there are no gays on the ship."

"Don't ask; don't tell." Mark said.

"But you seem to be saying if there *were* any, discipline would be ruined." She leaned back in the chair smiling.

In a way she was right, he conceded, but her view was too simplistic. He tried another argument. "What I'm talking about, I mean about ruining discipline — that happens *when* they're discovered. When it all comes to light, the crew gets worried." He knew there was something wrong with what he said, missing logic. Lynn would spot it instantly. He seldom outwitted her if his position was not on solid granite.

"Did you hear what you just said?" Lynn cocked her head and eyed him with her victory smile. "It's not the homosexuals who cause the discipline problems, it's the people who discover them! Ha! On that basis you ought to leave them alone. That will solve all your problems."

She was so damned exasperating. The principle certainly seemed sound when she said it, but he knew he could never advance the same argument to the captain. She wasn't thinking by the rules.

"Besides, what's wrong with gays in the Navy? Seems the crew, at least part of the crew, would be happier on long cruises."

He knew she was serious though she made her suggestion lightly. But how can you have guys diddling each other and not screw up morale? Maybe we can't keep all the gays out but we can damn sure make them scared to come out.

They cleared the table. As Mark scrubbed the sauce from the silverware, she stood next to him, taking the utensils from the rinse water one by one, dropping them into a draining rack.

He still had nothing, and the ship would be going to sea in a few days for a week of local-area gunfire exercises, towing a target ship. Impossible to get much done at sea with a pair of four-hour bridge watches every day on top of the regular office routine.

"Coming over tonight?"

"No, honey. I've got to spend some time on this damned case."

"You're not mad about our discussion, are you?"

"Of course not," he said, then quietly, "but you did get me to thinking. Don't see any way I can get around prosecuting without putting my own job on the line."

She tensed. "Is that all you can think about? Your career. I get so tired of hearing nothing but Navy this and Navy that. And that cutesy jargon that goes with it: 'Cover your ass,' 'Kick ass and take names,' 'Kiss ass.' You guys are so preoccupied with each other's ass, it's a wonder they don't throw you all out for being queer."

They stared at each other, something passing between them they had not known before. Her eyes flashed resentment. For the Navy? he wondered. Or for me?

The seconds passed slowly. He reached for her hand and she allowed him to draw her close.

"I can't blame you for feeling that way," he said. "It doesn't feel the same to me anymore either. But I'm close to forty and if I don't make lieutenant commander, I'll be out of the service with nothing. No retirement . . ." He stopped. She'd heard all this before. Just like he'd heard how Tony treated her, more times than he could remember. "I love you, Lynn. I don't want the Navy to break us up."

"I know," she said, turning back to the counter, placing her hands against it.

"Something wrong?"

"No, nothing," she said, allowing a smile to come to her lips.

Mark carried Vicky on his arms held straight out before him, like a robot delivering a sacrificial virgin. It was one of their games, and she woke long enough to squirm close to his chest and hug his neck. He lowered her into Lynn's Honda and buckled the strap around her. Every time he saw her sleeping, he felt a pang of loss that he had never had children of his own — Cora's vanity, her fear of aging. Initially she had tried talking him into getting a vasectomy so she could go off the pill — made her fat, she said.

Now, he watched Vicky, chin on her chest, cheeks puffed out with traces of barbecue sauce still around her lips. Another man's child, but he could love her. He would marry Lynn in a minute if only she would let him.

"See you tomorrow?"

"Oh no, Mark. Vicky has a play at school tomorrow evening, you know, the Spring Gala we've been working on. Tony will be there." She caught his disappointed look. "Sorry, she *is* his daughter. He does have a right to see the play. And I suppose he will want to take her out for ice cream later."

"How about the next night then, Thursday. I'm going to sea Friday morning for a week, maybe two — it'll depend on how fast the firing ships get through their exercises."

"Sure, see you Thursday then," she said, lowering herself into the seat. "Haven't they heard of weekends?"

★

Nine o'clock. Mark flipped on the television. The movie was a made-for-TV piece of fluff starring a twenty-year-old kid trying to act like a hard-bitten detective. He snapped the set off and scanned the room. He could have been at Motel 6. On the shelf, a few books he had already read — the new ones he bought at the Navy Exchange went directly to his stateroom aboard ship. No music except the radio — tapes all on the ship. Nothing else to read except Vicky's books, and he already had them practically memorized.

He poured a brandy and stared at the darkened television screen. Something's going wrong with my life, he thought as he drained the glass in a gulp and poured another. He hadn't gone with Lynn tonight because he knew their gays-in-the-Navy conversation would have continued — and he wasn't up to it, didn't have her enthusiasm for debate. He didn't have to think about Lamm. Quite the opposite, he didn't want to think at all. Still, Lynn's arguments kept coming back; still, he tried to reject them.

After his fourth brandy, he went to bed.

✯ Chapter Six ✯

Sir, I decided I want a lawyer and that I'm not going to make any kind of statement until I get advice," Lamm said, speaking softly but with an underlying intensity.

Mark regarded the petty officer for a moment, noticing Lamm's quiet demeanor. "I think that's wise. The legal center wants referrals from command legal officers, though — won't take walk-ins. I'll call for an appointment for you."

He watched Lamm tightly grip his white hat. He wanted to talk, that was clear, but he wouldn't. Petty Officer Marion Lamm followed rules, knew discipline. He wasn't like some of the young sailors who, when called before authority, waived all their rights after a moment and confessed to Mark, as if to their mothers, through a veil of tears. The child-sailors made it disgustingly easy to prosecute them, writing their own guilty verdicts. Good for the captain, too. He didn't have to make a decision about their guilt and could sentence them immediately. He usually hit them with the maximum he could at mast. Take a stripe, half their pay for two months, and restrict them to the ship. If he did less, the sailors felt he had been particularly benevolent and could be heard calling him a "fair man, tough, but fair."

Lamm's no fool, Mark thought. He wouldn't make it easy for them to crush his career. He must also know he hasn't a pissant's chance in a firestorm of beating the system. "I'll let you know about the appointment soon as I can."

"Lieutenant, about Overmiller . . . I never touched him. That's the truth. Even if I was a queer, why would I hit on a sailor I didn't know about, particularly one in my own division?"

Against his better judgment, Mark spoke. "I don't know what the truth is about all this, Petty Officer Lamm. I'm trying to find out, trying to end it satisfactorily."

"For who? Overmiller tells a lie and my life falls apart. How do I stop my men from thinking about it? How do I stop the rumors?"

"There are procedures for handling this and that's what I'm doing, Petty Officer Lamm. That's what I'm doing," Mark said, voice raising in volume.

"What are the procedures for getting my respect back, to make the men stop laughing behind my back? What are those procedures, Lieutenant?"

Mark stood and pushed the chair back. "You'd better leave now. You aren't helping yourself here."

Lamm paused at the door for a moment, staring at Mark, as if seeing his enemy for the first time, identifying Mark as the instrument, the weapon that would cut him down.

Mark felt the difference in Lamm — fear, frustration and a will to fight. For an instant Mark wanted desperately for Lamm to say something that would make it right. Of course he knew that was foolish, impossible. Why should the accused offer the prosecutor succor, comfort?

"Thanks, Lieutenant," Lamm said without rancor. For a moment, the two men were boxers touching gloves. Then Lamm slipped out the door, closing it quietly.

Last night's brandy fought for control of Mark's skull as he flopped on his bunk. Too early for his regular fifteen minutes of morning think time, but he didn't care at the moment. The doorknob was adjacent to the foot of his bed and he flipped the lock with the toe of his Corfam.

What would I do in Lamm's place? he wondered. It could just as easily have been me. Probably not as likely, but the process would be the same. Well, not exactly the same. It would be quiet. I'd leave the ship and stay at home, calling in to muster once a day until the paperwork allowing me to resign my commission was completed.

Gentle, civilized, with a modicum of grace and as little embarrassment as possible for all concerned. Of course I'd be expected to be quiet, too. No lawyers or hearings, no press. *For the good of the service.* Lamm, on the other hand, would be assigned a lowly job on the ship, a pariah. Psychological punishment. It was never enough to simply discharge an enlisted. The Navy had to extract a price.

The phone shook him from his bunk and he lunged across the room to catch up the handset before it could jangle a second time.

"Mark. Come on up."

"Yes, sir," he said to a dead line. The skipper and his fake Gary Cooper terseness, he thought. Never would say what it was about. On instinct, he snatched the case file and Lamm's personnel record off the desk and planted them tightly between his elbow and his side, cradling the corner with his palm. He liked to think it was the way Alec Guinness carried his swagger stick in *The Bridge on the River Kwai.* He knew it made him look sharp and purposeful even though his neck ached and his head throbbed.

★

"I want him off this ship before we leave for Long Beach."

"But why, sir?"

"I think that's obvious, Mark," the captain said levelly, eyeing him as though he had expected protest.

"What I mean is that unless he's done something I don't know about, it would be tough justifying. The other thing is, Dave needs him badly in engineering."

"Why am I getting excuses from you instead of action? Why do you keep finding reasons why something can't be done rather than simply doing it?" Bennett spoke as though Mark were a teenager and the subject a messy bedroom.

"Captain," Mark began, swallowing his urge to lash out, "we're dealing in an area that could backfire on us very easily. Lamm has only been accused. There is virtually no evidence. He's certainly not dangerous to himself or to the crew so the brig is out — even for pretrial confinement. We can't force him to use accumulated leave, and to just plunk him ashore would prejudice any case we could build. Even the Secretary of the Navy's instruction on admin discharges specifies in homosexual cases the man *has* to be kept on board until word comes back from the bureau to discharge —"

Bennett slapped the desk. "Excuses!"

Regulations! Mark resisted the urge to snap at the captain and drew a slow breath. "I suppose I could try to send him on temporary assignment somewhere. Shore Patrol is out. They won't take anyone accused of a Justice Code violation. Special services, maybe, but really,

Skipper, with manning at about eighty percent we'd be cutting our own throats to lose his talents — especially at sea."

"Are you willing to take responsibility for his actions during the sea period?" Bennett asked.

"How can I be responsible for someone I can't control? I can't even say good morning without reading him his rights first. He's Dave Brown's man. Maybe Dave should have a chance to answer the question since it affects his workload." Mark felt he had turned the heat in another direction while at the same time looking out for Dave's interests. Hadn't he said at lunch he couldn't afford to lose Lamm?

"All right, Mark. We'll do it your way. I'm pretty sure I know what our chief engineer will say since he's always crying for more bodies. But I don't like the idea one bit. How's it shaping up otherwise?"

"Not good, sir. The search came up negative — that's what the report from Special Agent Berquist said — though to watch him you'd think he stumbled onto Mafia headquarters. Found some uniforms in a closet that really got him going."

"Uniforms?"

"Berquist said homosexuals like to dress up in uniforms and go to gay bars." Mark instantly wished he hadn't mentioned it.

Bennett raised in his chair, fists gripping the arms. Mark interpreted the horrified look on the captain's face and quickly continued. "Not *Navy* uniforms. They were like for gas stations, security guards, that kind of uniform."

Bennett sat back. "Trouble is, the uniforms don't mean anything as evidence," Mark continued. "Not much question that Overmiller was there. His statement describes the layout of the apartment accurately and there was a porno tape there that matches what he said he saw. Oh, and this one other thing. There were two men in Lamm's apartment when we went in. One sleeping on the couch and the other was in his skivvies like he'd just got up."

Bennett's eyes lit.

"I tried to talk with them. Civilians. Clammed up right away. No jurisdiction. Couldn't force them."

"What is their connection to Lamm?"

"Still don't know except that I think one of them lives there and the other was staying temporarily, one or two nights. Figured that from overhearing them talk to each other. Tried to take a statement from Lamm this morning, but he wants a lawyer first. I was just about to make an appointment for him when you called."

"So what do we have?"

"Not nearly enough for a court-martial, sir. Sorry. Looks like we're stuck with an admin discharge board."

"That's what you wanted all along, isn't it?" the captain said, kicking the corner of his desk with the toe of his shoe, one leg crossed over the other.

"No, sir," Mark answered, standing stiffer, fingernails digging into palms, muscles tightened as if for attack.

"Well, isn't it true that you would be the prosecutor on this admin board? And you want to play Perry Mason."

Mark's contempt for the captain grew and he seized on his trivial error — Perry Mason was a *defense* attorney — to further justify his dislike of the man.

"No sir. I don't. Lamm will have a real lawyer on his side and I don't relish the thought of going head to head with a JAG officer." But he couldn't deny being intrigued by the idea. There was a certain appeal in the scene — the opposing attorney flummoxed by his brilliant argument, congratulating Mark on his victory. There'd be no shame in losing the case to a real lawyer, either. He knew, though, that if Bennett thought he would enjoy being the recorder, the prosecutor, the captain would never go along with it easily. He liked to see his officers sweat, excel against the odds, vanquish fear. His words.

"All right then, let's go with the admin board. I suppose that's the only way." The captain selected a corncob pipe from the rack and began stuffing strings of tobacco into the bowl. "And send Dave Brown in here, would you?"

"Yes, sir. Anything else, Skipper?" Mark maintained his passive expression.

"Just one thing. I'm looking for an opponent now that the XO is retiring. Do you play chess?"

Mark glanced at the small table with onyx board and chessmen perennially on display and imagined facing Bennett hours on end. He thought of the hours he had spent as a teenager with a neighbor over a similar board. The retired civil engineer had come as close as any man to providing Mark a father figure.

"No, sir. Never learned the game," he said. The game meant too much to him to share with someone he liked as little as the captain.

★

"Just a moment," the female voice said, "I'll connect you with Lieutenant Templeman in Defense Division."

Waiting on hold, Mark took the moment to think about Lynn. He couldn't fathom why she balked at deepening their relationship, coming out of the closet, so to speak. He knew the reasons she recited, had them memorized, but while they apparently satisfied her they came off to him as inadequate. The whole damned mess frustrated him, and sometimes he thought he should just chuck it all with her, find a different girlfriend, at least a woman with different problems.

But he couldn't. He loved her.

So he took the frustration of a relationship on hold one day at a time and tried not to think of the two years that would have to pass before she'd be able to get out from under Tony's influence.

"Lieutenant Templeman." The voice identified its owner, jerking Mark back from his daydream.

"This is Lieutenant Palmer, Legal Officer on *Modoc.* I need an appointment for one of our people to arrange for defense. It's an admin discharge board for homosexual harassment."

"Name?"

"Mine or his?"

"His," the voice said flatly, unperturbed, unlike most in the Navy who dealt constantly over the phone and expected everyone else to know exactly what they meant.

"Lamm, Marion Arthur." He spelled it using the phonetic alphabet. "Lima, Alfa, Mike, Mike . . ."

"Whew," Templeman said when Mark gave Lamm's rank as Machinist's Mate First Class. "First class, huh? It's usually the junior people who show up before a board."

"We are going to sea Friday morning. Could you see him today or tomorrow?"

"Sure. I'll need to see his record and duplicates of your evidence. Have you informed him yet?"

"Only that he was charged. The skipper just decided on the board a moment ago. I haven't put the letter of notification together yet but I'll let him know before I send him over."

The paperwork would be mountainous.

"How about 1400 today?"

"That's great. Thanks, he'll be there."

He pressed the button to disconnect and dialed again, an off-base number. Tom LaCroix, his sea daddy — his shipboard mentor and friend when Mark was assigned as a new officer. Mark thought of Tom as a truly happy man — single, retired from the Navy, writing a novel, caring not one whit about convention.

"Yello!" Tom answered.

"So how's life in the shitcan Navy?"

"Mark? That you Looouten-ant? You checkin' to see if I've croaked yet?" Tom routinely chided Mark about the notion that sailors die soon after leaving the Navy. The all-encompassing belief held that retirees having no spot in the chain of command couldn't live long. It took the story of one chief petty officer's fatal heart attack on the golf course the day after his retirement party to establish the thought as gospel. Anyone surviving past that point was merely an exception living on borrowed time.

"Doing anything tonight, Tom? Let me buy you dinner at the Harbor House."

"Got a problem, Mark?" The voice was suddenly conciliatory.

"You can tell, huh?"

"Come on, admit it. The dinner is a payoff."

"Could use a powwow, pal," Mark admitted.

"Like I always said: 'A friend in need is a pain in the ass.' But dinner's not necessary."

"Well, we both have to eat, and I've been wondering if you've learned any manners yet."

A belch was Tom's only answer.

★

Tom LaCroix had shown Mark an Orient he'd never seen before when they served together on the aircraft carrier, USS *Ranger.* He'd introduced Mark to fried ice cream at Jimmy's Kitchen in Hong Kong and Rothschild's Bordeaux at the Peninsula Hotel in Kowloon. At Pattaya Beach, Thailand, it was the massage parlor where nude women scrubbed and soaped them until their bodies looked like they'd been plucked from a washing machine before the rinse cycle. Then, on soapy air mattresses the dark girls squirmed on top of the men, pressing their small breasts between foamy buttocks, dragging stiff pubic patches up the men's legs.

Tom laughed, the girls laughed, when Mark, unable to stand the erotic tension, came into the rounded plastic terrain of the air mattress between two rolls, like a miniature ass. He had concealed his embarrassment and laughed with them when he finally caught his breath. He rolled over as he felt the soap begin to dry on his back and held his penis limply, gesturing as though it had let him down, scolding it, keeping the joke going in sign language for the benefit of the Thai-speaking girls.

Later he thought about the embarrassment he felt not only for losing control, but for having ejaculated in Tom's presence — mostly for the latter.

One evening Tom spoke about what he sensed had been bothering the younger officer as they shared a pair of *Singha* beers in a Pattaya Beach open-air bar. "Suppose you feel a little funny about what happened at that massage joint." He went on without waiting for an answer. "My first time there I damn near glued myself to the mattress. Sensory overload. If you've never felt anything like that before, your balls take over. Don't worry about it, I have it on good authority the girls have a pool. The one sexy enough to bring a guy off without ever touching his cock gets to collect. Everybody wins that way.

"You did the right thing, boy *san.* Make it a joke. Sex is a joke anyway. Ever look at it from a nonerotic standpoint? Try it sometime. Funny as hell it is. All that bare skin flapping and slapping, the moaning." While Tom did a falsetto imitation of skin-flick dialog, Mark looked nervously around the bar, wondering if anyone had heard, if anyone cared.

"Really stupid looking." Tom chuckled. He let his laughter fade, then put one hand on Mark's arm. "Don't misunderstand what I'm going to say, but it was nice to watch you. I mean you were having a good time, hell, the ultimate good time. I was glad to see you cut loose, find out it's all right to have some fun. I was happy for you, really. Know what I mean?"

Mark knew what he meant. He really cared for Tom, though he hesitated to think *love.* But the attraction, their easy compatibility, frightened him from getting too close and he was sure Tom felt it, too. What Tom had said came closest to an admission. Mark thought of the way the mattress felt against his cock, the pair of rolls — the miniature ass — and wondered what it meant about him. That scared him, too. He knew he shouldn't have liked it so much.

Neither officer mentioned the incident again.

☆ CHAPTER SEVEN ☆

MARK GAZED at the massive black-painted hull of the schooner, *Star of India,* now a maritime museum, in its berth at San Diego's Broadway pier. The tall ship also served as Mark's place to think. He ignored the tourists clattering up the gangway and concentrated on the play of water-reflected sunlight against the rough plating. He wanted to reach out across the span of water, touch the metal. Some strange force drew him to the engineless ship. He imagined her at sea, relying on the wind and her men. The steel-banded wooden masts and rigging were silhouetted against the bright sky. In his mind's eye sailors climbed the masts and scrambled along the spars to secure billowing canvas in place.

The *Star* spoke peacefully to him and he would spend the odd moment — like these few minutes before meeting Tom — listening, watching from the pier. A place to collect his thoughts: Lynn, his career, and now Lamm.

Tom would be driving from his place in Coronado across the sweeping, curved bridge over San Diego Bay. Tom referred to his apartment as a windowless garret in the hope it would help his image as a writer — a tongue-in-cheek statement, like most he made. Mark had learned to tell the difference after the nine-month cruise aboard *Ranger* as Tom's roommate.

Seaport Village — San Diego's waterfront theme mall a few blocks down Harbor Drive from the *Star of India* — held no interest for Mark save the Harbor House, his favorite restaurant. The eclectic collection of modern buildings, designed to look turn-of-the-century, had the charm of a Spanish fishing village and the convenience of clean restrooms. A shopper's Disneyland.

He met Tom at the Harbor House desk, then walked to the bar on the upper deck, a perch for daytime people-watching and evening body swaps. They ordered drinks from a cocktail waitress whose side-slit skirt captured the attention of them both.

Retirement — far from being sudden death — agreed with Tom LaCroix. Mark noticed an increasingly casual look about his friend. He had taken to boatneck pullovers and Levi's and seldom wore socks. Now, as they occupied one of the low couches by the tall windows watching the sun set over Coronado, he could detect an easy sophistication in his former shipmate he'd not noticed before. Tom had jettisoned the tension that permeates a Navy junior officer's life. He now moved fluidly and spoke with candor.

"How's the writing going? Keeping you in beans?"

Tom laughed in his characteristic way, not a hearty belly laugh, more a heh-heh, sly-sounding chuckle. "If I had to rely on writing for food I'd grow cobwebs in my asshole. The retirement check mostly takes care of that.

"Well," he said, suddenly modest, "I did sell an article to *Popular Mechanics*. A comparison shopper's guide to paintbrushes."

"What issue? I'll look for it."

Tom laughed and patted Mark's shoulder. "You

really would, wouldn't you. Just pulling your leg. No, I'm still plugging away on the great American epic. So far I've gotten the protagonist up to ten years old and he still hasn't lost his cherry. Looks like it'll be a long book." He sipped a glass of white wine and cocked his ear as "Palmer, party of two" was announced.

Mark left the dinner wine choice up to Tom. All he knew was they'd be sharing a bottle from bin 31.

"Tom," he began, feeling the conversational amenities had been completed, "I could use your thoughts on a couple of problems. Well, not really problems. Let's say situations."

"Why not just spit it out? Makes me nervous to watch you wriggle around like a salamander on a hot plate."

Had he forgotten who he was with? "My love life is the pits and I'm ready to strangle the captain."

He explained his problems with Lynn, stopping only when the wine, a Santa Ynez Valley Chardonnay, arrived and Tom discussed its merits with the steward.

"Where was I . . ." Mark said, testing whether Tom had been paying attention.

"Two more years before Lynn will be free of the yoke of oppression," Tom answered without a moment's hesitation. "Don't worry, I've been listening. Never can tell when a new plot idea will pop up."

"I don't know what to do about it in the meantime. I don't want to stop living for two years."

"Sounds like an adjustment rather than a matter of stopping or starting."

"But I don't want to wait all that time to get our life together. They're divorced, so it seems unfair that she'd let Tony still have control over the relationship."

"So what are you going to do while Lynn is on cruise?"

"Huh?"

"Cruise. On cruise. Deployed, away. The irony seems rather clear. It's beyond her control, *she* says, and you're stuck waiting on the pier until she gets back to you. Only you don't know if it will be a six-month cruise or a nine-month cruise or if she'll *ever* return. How does it feel to be a WestPac widow?"

"Sucks." Mark looked away from the table. Tom was right. Lynn was the problem. She didn't have to knuckle under to Tony.

"Look, if this is too tough for you I could lie for a while. Or . . . we could talk pork bellies and soybean futures."

"No," was all Mark could say as the thoughts raced through his mind, feeling around the edges of this new perspective.

The server arrived. Mark ordinarily relished the monkfish in a lightly seasoned lemon sauce but now he couldn't concentrate on the taste and swallowed mechanically. He looked up to catch Tom watching him while idly poking at his own order of bay scallops.

"Pardon me," Mark said. "Have I been pouting?"

"Not too badly, but they are passing a sympathy card around the tables. Everyone's signing it."

"Sorry, Tom. It's not every day I get clobbered with the truth."

"You may still be missing the point, boy *san.* It doesn't do any good to whip yourself about this. You and Lynn are simply on divergent paths. They may come together somewhere down the line, in two years or twenty. I think you're feeling down now because you want a woman to rely on, go home to at night. She isn't the one. Not now." Tom scooped a few scallops from the sauce and chewed slowly. "Of course, there may be something she has you don't want to lose for even a few years. Then you have to examine whether it's important enough for you to be without her now and then — while she's on cruise."

Mark wondered if he would be able to give Lynn the same loyalty he expected from her while he was at sea.

"Look," Tom said, "I don't know Lynn from Adam's off ox, but I think I know you. Sure, I may have been feeding you a line of bullshit just now, but I don't think so." He held up a hand to silence Mark. "Don't say anything about it now. Think. You'll know what the answer is. Then I'll send my bill." He speared a scallop.

★

In the morning Mark took his place in the officer ranks on *Modoc*'s fantail. Morning quarters. The crew stood at attention while the old man talked about water conservation during the coming sea period. "The new paradigm for water use calls for a robust adherence to the ship's conservation policy . . ."

Bullshit. Mark watched the public Bennett as he used too many buzzwords, too many times — Beltway clichés he picked up from *C-SPAN* and the Sunday television talking heads.

Mark knew the next thing would be for the captain to call him forward to pin a medal on him, but his mind was on the dollop of grease he'd picked off a valve stem in the 0–1 passageway with his khaki shirtsleeve.

The captain loved to spring award presentations on the crew, catch them unaware, whenever he had a chance. Mark knew about his own medal because his office handled awards when notification came in from Washington. He had been given orders that the men never be told beforehand.

Mark stopped smartly in front of the small portable lectern that contained its own loudspeaker. He saluted and stood at attention while Bennett read the citation in his theatrical voice. The speaker on the lectern allowed him full range of his vocal cords, from a whisper to a bellow. But the speaker hummed with each sweep of radar from passing ships, mercifully obscuring some of the captain's words.

"The Secretary of the Navy takes pleasure in presenting the Navy Commendation Medal to Mark A. Palmer, Lieutenant, United States Navy, for service as set forth in the following citation: For meritorious achievement while serving as assistant officer in charge of Pacific Intelligence Collection Team . . ."

Mark wondered what the men standing in formation on the fantail really thought about his being up there, waiting to be pinned with a medal. He remembered how he felt when he had been enlisted — proud to serve with a medal winner, secure in knowing a shipmate had proven dependable. He didn't believe that today the men felt as he had witnessing his first awards ceremony nearly twenty years before; much had changed. He had to admit his feelings had changed as well. Commanding officers were no longer unapproachable godlike creatures, dispensers of justice and wisdom. They were just officers further up the ladder. One day he would, himself, wear the command star on his pocket — *if* he could avoid another tour on a backwater tub like *Modoc* and survive the Lamm case.

". . . resulting in a significant improvement in Pacific Fleet intelligence collection. On his own initiative, he sought advanced technical computer information from outside the Navy intelligence community and applied . . ."

He was getting a little old. Six years as a photographic intelligence interpreter, four more years in college earning his degree under a Navy engineering education program, commissioning as an ensign and his first assignment as main propulsion assistant on a guided missile cruiser. Then came the aircraft carrier engineering assignment, and then the intelligence team — and now *Modoc.*

Mark's experience as an enlisted intelligence specialist had qualified him for the team — a plum job for a junior officer. Now, as he was reminded of it, he wished he had been able to stay there — to avoid the Lamm mess and the dead-dull routine of *Modoc.* He didn't even have an engineering job anymore. How he would love to return to the intelligence team where they joked that their work schedule was written in Moscow because any suspicious Russian naval activity triggered the small, fast-moving group into action. Equipped with high-resolution cameras and film, P-3 Orion patrol aircraft ferried them, flying low over the target ships that were themselves collecting intelligence. *Trawlers* the US press called the Russian vessels. Loitering off the coast, the only trawling they did with their elaborate antenna suite was for American and NATO communications.

The Santa Ana wind snapped the flag on the jackstaff. The men clutched at their hats, denying the hot flow from the desert an opportunity to fling them into San Diego Harbor. Their upraised arms would be forgiven, though they were supposed to be at attention. Remembering the loss of his own white hat to wind, Mark recalled the chewing out he had gotten from his division chief so long ago. *"What do you MEAN, the wind got it? The proper hat size screwed on tight won't blow away, Palmer. Your only excuse is an improper fitting uniform and I don't want no sailors in my division that can't wear a proper uniform!"*

The man had been a martinet. Mark had not understood then why he reacted as he did to the unwarranted tirade. He had grown deeper in his resolve to please the chief, even when witnesses to the incident encouraged him to slash the old bastard's tires.

". . . professionalism and devotion to duty reflected great credit on himself and were in keeping with the highest traditions of the United States Naval Service.

"For the Secretary of the Navy, signed P. R. Parker, Admiral, U.S. Navy, Commander in Chief, U.S. Pacific Fleet."

Commander Bennett closed the blue plastic cover over the citation and held the medal dangling on a green and white ribbon at arm's length for the ranks to see. He walked around the lectern and paused while an open look of pride settled on his wide face — a father surveying a graduating son. He pinned the medal crookedly on Mark's khaki shirt pocket, gripped his hand for an exaggerated shake and stepped back a pace.

"Post!" he commanded.

Mark saluted, holding until Bennett returned the gesture, then executed an about-face and marched back to the gap in the officer rank between Frank Madera and Dave Brown. Frank's eyes were closed and he weaved in the wind, humming tunelessly, his imminent retirement obviously his only thought.

★

In the cramped wardroom following quarters the other officers slapped Mark on the back and shook his hand, inspecting the new ornament hanging on his shirt.

"How many terrorists you have to waste for that one?" Dave Brown asked. "Think that's going to help you get my job?"

"What? And get my uniforms filthy? Hell no, you keep it," Mark answered, though the truth was if things got worse with Bennett he'd be glad for any job beside legal officer.

A mess cook leaned over Mark's shoulder. "Lieutenant Palmer, CO is on the phone for you."

"Congratulations again, Mark," Bennett said quickly, as if he hadn't pinned the medal on him a half-hour earlier, "Come up to my cabin pronto."

"Aye aye, sir." He knew he could get by without the "aye aye," but it seemed to help set his mood for whatever might be coming. His moment of glory had already faded and it was back to business as usual.

Bennett let Mark stand. "I've thought about this admin board and, while I can't prove anything, I have the feeling you're trying to skizzle me."

The captain paused, studying Mark. "I expect you to win this admin board. I want the man out with an other-than-honorable discharge. My endorsement will simply be that I concur with the board's findings. Do you understand that?"

"Yes, sir."

"You're not going to make me the heavy on this."

"Sir, I will be going against a lawyer . . ."

"And you think that's a convenient excuse for losing the case? Well, mister, I say that you will simply have to prepare a better presentation than the lawyer does. Convince the board that Lamm is scum. You can say anything you want. Don't have to prove a thing."

"Captain, are you asking me to lie before the board?"

Bennett paused as color rushed to his face. "I'm telling you to win this case. At the end of it, Lamm will be out or you will be." He slammed his open palm on the desk. "I'll fix it so you'll never make lieutenant commander. You better learn quick that my officers follow orders! I've been watching you. I've seen how you operate and I'm calling an end to it right now. You understand?"

"No, sir, I really don't." The hair prickled on Mark's neck and he moved inches toward Bennett, leaning forward. He squeezed the words between his teeth, "I've been doing my job. You just gave me a medal."

"That was from your *last* job! I require more than a *job* from my officers, mister. I require spirit, loyalty and *truth.*"

Bennett drew Mark's personnel file from his desk and flipped it open to the page marked ENLISTED CLASSIFICATION RECORD — a twenty-year-old form carried over from his original enlisted record. "Read what this says."

Mark hesitated.

"Goddamnit, I said read."

Mark stepped forward and peered at the word Bennett underlined with his finger in the box labeled LEISURE TIME ACTIVITIES. His throat tightened.

"Read it!"

"Chess. It says chess."

"Is that your signature at the bottom?"

He knew damned well it was. "Yes, sir."

"You told me you never learned the game. That makes you a liar, doesn't it?" A smile cracked the corners of Bennett's mouth.

☆ Chapter Eight ☆

The churning in Mark's gut had slowed by the time he reached his stateroom. Now as he lay in his bunk staring at the pipes running along the overhead, it felt dead, an empty space between his heart and his butt. Exposed in a lie to the commanding officer. No matter it was only a small one about something as inconsequential as whether he played chess. He *had* lied — and Bennett knew. That knowledge placed the guillotine trip lever in the captain's hands.

The irony of it all — he never lied about important things. He tried to remember the exact conversation. *"Mark, do you play chess?" "No, sir, I never learned."* If he had only said "No, sir," and had left it at that then it wouldn't have been a lie.

He let the argument slip away. No point. What really happened or what might have happened didn't matter — only what Bennett believed made any difference.

Mark stayed in his stateroom the rest of the day poring over paperwork necessary to get the admin board established and officially request counsel for Lamm from the legal center. The work had to be completed anyway, but it gave him a convenient excuse to avoid the other officers. They couldn't know about his confrontation with Bennett — but he knew. Besides, he'd have to face them all for an inescapable week at sea starting in the morning. At least he'd have the night with Lynn. Any luck and it would be better than his day.

★

Vicky spotted his car from the tiny playground near the apartment and ran screeching to meet him. Mark hoisted her to his shoulders and she wrapped her arms around his head, dribbling sand from her overalls into his hair and down his shirt. Lynn met them at the door and sent Vicky back down the stairs to play once her excitement over Mark's arrival had deteriorated after five minutes to disinterest.

"So how was the spring concert?" he asked.

"Spring Gala," she corrected, "It was fine. Vicky remembered both her lines, vernal *and* equinox."

"Tony make it?"

"Of course. He wouldn't miss it, the jerk."

"Any trouble?"

"Just the usual. What did you do with yourself?"

She changed the subject. He was just as glad, since talk of Tony always depressed them both. He tried to avoid bringing up Tony's name because when Lynn started firing salvos about her ex, Mark usually took a few unintended hits as well.

Along with everyone else in uniform, Mark had been assigned to one of the Navy's sensitivity courses the year before and had met Captain Tony Gianelli there. Since the Tailhook sex scandal, the services had taken remedial action to quell the media furor. Tony had been smart and funny in class. In spite of Lynn's undisguised disdain for her ex-husband, Mark had liked the senior officer, making him feel guilty now.

"Had dinner with Tom LaCroix," he answered Lynn now.

"I wonder about you two. You spent forever on the carrier together and you still see each other. Strange for Navy. Nobody sees anyone after a transfer. What's so special about him?"

"He's my friend . . . and what's got you so bitchy? You have friends, why shouldn't I?"

"Sorry. I didn't mean it to sound that way. You just never seem to cultivate friends."

Now he *was* getting depressed. First Bennett, now Lynn. "Listen to us, chipping away at each other. Look, I love you, want to be with you." He held her shoulders and their eyes met, exchanging the feeling that they were, indeed, in love. No mistaking that. They embraced, and the pressures of *Modoc* and Bennett drained from his mind. Lynn had that effect. When she opened her arms to him, little else mattered.

After dinner and Mark reading Vicky to sleep, they undressed and made love slowly; it would be the last time for a week. Afterward he drew the sheet from her breasts and stroked them. From outside across the court, sounds of a party reached them, filtered by the gently moving bedroom draperies. A siren howled far away and, closer, crickets sounded like tiny unoiled hinges. They lay touching at the hips and her hand traced a pattern on his chest.

"Something bothering you?" she said softly.

"Nothing."

She always knew. She said once she could tell by his eyes and the way he talked — quietly, slowly, choosing each word, afraid that an inappropriate phrase would make things worse. Whenever she asked, he answered, "Nothing." A reflex. In a few minutes her silence drew him out.

"Bennett asked me if I played chess. I told him I had never learned. So he drags out a personal data sheet from my enlisted record where I had listed chess as a leisure activity. Now he's using it to pressure me into making up evidence in the Lamm case since it's so weak."

"Lamm is the homosexual?"

"Accused. I don't know if I can prove the charges, not even sure I believe them." He rolled onto his back, cradled his head in his hands, and sighed.

Lynn watched him in silence for a moment then padded softly into the kitchen, returning with a pair of snifters and her bottle of Christmas brandy.

He sat up against the pillow. "Special occasion?" he asked, knowing that particular bottle had cost thirty-two dollars and wasn't often uncorked.

She poured and handed him a glass. "Sounds like you could use it."

They could smell a barbecue outside and hear party noises. Things were normal out there.

"So what will you do?"

"Carry out my orders." He gave a rueful laugh. "Don't have much choice if I ever expect to finish my career."

"I know it is important to you but is that what you want — after this?"

"It's just a matter of surviving Bennett for another year. When he leaves the ship it'll be better."

"I've heard that before — everyone's always waiting for orders, their own or someone else's. Are you sure it's just Bennett?"

"It has to be. Nothing like this has ever happened before. He's just a fluke."

"But what about Lamm? How's he come out in this? Are you just going to railroad him out?"

"I've got to find the proof, that's all."

"And if you don't?"

★

Mark stood on the starboard wing — the open bit of deck beside the pilothouse. "Single up all lines," he said.

The phone talker repeated his command into the microphone slung against his chest. Below, the line handlers slipped one of the two sets of mooring lines from the bollards on the quay.

Mark checked the engine room's response to his commands. He couldn't afford to have anything go wrong this morning. He'd taken *Modoc* and much larger ships out before, but it hadn't been his turn today. Captain Bennett had changed the rotation. He would be watching carefully from his canvas director's chair on the signal bridge. Mark could hear the captain's scraping and coughing above him but refused to look up. He felt Bennett's eyes on his back, watching for the slightest mistake which he could loudly correct — for the immediate safety of the ship, of course — and to which Mark's response would have to be, "Aye aye, sir."

"Cast off all lines," he said to the talker loud enough for the rest of the bridge watch to hear. He ordered *Modoc*'s twin propellers spun in opposite directions and the bow swung away from the pier.

"All engines ahead one-third."

The helmsman swung the engine room telegraph lever around and back to one-third, jangling a bell. The pointer beneath, like a clock's hour hand, made the same movement, and the thrashing propellers bit water.

"Helm, come five degrees to port."

"Aye aye, sir. Helm is five degrees to port."

"Rudder amidships," he ordered immediately.

"Aye aye, sir. Rudder is amidships."

Modoc swung gently to the center of the opening between the long piers and the ships tied there, moving toward the main channel. Going to sea was the thing Mark loved most about the Navy, driving the ship and feeling it move beneath him, responding to his orders. At sea he could settle into his routine of watches, sleep, and work. Sea time was his opiate. The rest of the world disappeared, didn't count, and in his imagination, Lynn could be any woman he wanted.

The hard part was finished, a successful maneuver in a tight space. He glanced up at the captain, who sat staring at the city's changing skyline. Mark knew he had performed properly.

"Now, sir?" he called up, immediately wishing he hadn't.

"Yes, Mister Palmer. This is usually the time. Oh, I forgot, you're new here."

Mark stepped inside. "Bo'sun, start the tape."

The sailor on watch grinned. "Aye aye, sir." He punched the PLAY button and switched the 1MC from ANNOUNCE to INPUT. He twisted the volume knob and "Ride of the Valkyries" boomed from the speakers on deck and in every compartment throughout the ship. It would continue on an endless tape loop until the ship cleared Ballast Point and passed the tip of Point Loma. The piece never failed to remind Mark of the movie line: "I love the smell of napalm in the morning."

Most of the crew was openly embarrassed by the music that had replaced the Sousa marches — which were bad enough. It started when Dave Brown had wrangled the loan of *Apocalypse Now* from the base movie exchange and the captain had seen the video at sea. The helicopter attack scene with Wagner's music blasting had made its mark.

Cruisers and destroyers, warships, leaving port played "Cat Scratch Fever" or ragtime, or Preservation Hall jazz. *Modoc* left port screaming blood and vengeance at a top speed of eleven knots with two twenty-millimeter machine guns on the bridge — if the lone gunner's mate happened to have overcome his embarrassment and hauled the puny pop guns up from storage to the pedestal mounts.

Mark turned the conn — full responsibility for navigation of *Modoc* — over to Chief Fenton, and went below to his stateroom. The swell and chop of the seas outside the protection of San Diego Harbor made for a rough ride in *Modoc*'s broadly curved hull. He never had a problem with motion and even lying in his bunk, feeling his belly go heavy, then light, with the rise and fall of the ship, was no bother. He rather liked it, like a carnival ride.

They would make Long Beach in the evening, pick up the tow — a decommissioned destroyer escort — the next morning, and move slowly back to an operations area west of San Diego for gunfire practice. A hull shoot. Sinking a ship. Should be something to see, he thought, the excitement of a sinking ship with no dead sailors. It appealed to him. Like a grand-scale demolition derby, like a Stallone movie. These days it was a rare sight because of strict environmental regulations — a hull to be sunk had to be pristine, containing no hazardous materials.

Dave Brown clomped down the passageway — Mark recognized the arrhythmic walk Dave attributed to a college basketball injury — and shouldered the door an instant before turning the handle, making it shudder in its frame. Dave stumbled in, a confused look across his face, and turned to study the door as though it had jumped unexpectedly into his path.

"They trust you with engines, huh?" Mark laughed, wishing secretly he could be the one so entrusted.

"Damned doors. Always in the wrong place," Dave countered lightly. "Like this on all Vietnam-era ships," he said, studying the door. "Primitive engineering." He put the issue to rest. "So how's the decimation going?"

"Huh?" Mark said, puzzled by the term and the cheerful sound of Dave's voice.

"Decimation. Decimation of my ranks. You know, Lamm."

Mark's anger flashed, "Don't start laying that shit on me, Dave. Remember it was one of your boys that brought the whole thing up."

"Take it easy," Dave said, holding his hands before him as if to fend off an attack dog. "I didn't mean anything." He stood uneasily when Mark turned back to his desk. Tension drew the air taut. Mark sucked a breath and rocked back in his chair.

"Sorry, Dave. It has me on edge. That's all. How's Lamm taking all this — speaking of being on edge."

"Hasn't changed his work a bit." Dave flopped on his bunk. "If anything, he seems more dedicated than before. I'm sure he thinks he can beat this thing. Lots of scuttlebutt — rumor mill has been churning — but who can really tell what it all means. Still, there might have been a problem brewing there. Had to take Overmiller out of A and E Division to keep the peace. I made him Chief Vega's gofer so Vega could keep an eye on him. Wish it were the other way around. Overmiller I could lose."

"Ever wonder about that? I mean how we're programmed to look at the truth. If Lamm had accused Overmiller, you'd be ready to believe it because Overmiller is a thorn in your side. Don't misunderstand me. I'm talking about all of us, me included. Easy to believe the worst of a dirtbag. Couldn't it just be possible Overmiller is telling the truth?"

"I can't afford to lose Lamm. I don't give a shit if he's queer or not."

"Good point, but you're evading the question of truth. What if Lamm *is* homosexual? SECNAV says we gotta throw him out."

Dave sat up. "Well, I suppose if it's proved beyond a shadow of a doubt that he propositioned a straight sailor, we'll have to follow regulations and discharge him."

"Wrong on two counts, and this is what's got me crossing swords with Bennett. Lamm doesn't have to be *proved* homosexual, just *believed* to be. Big difference there. And second, *we* won't have to discharge him. I'll have that chore."

"You really are pissed about not getting the chief engineer billet, aren't you? That's what this is all about — my job. You'd like to see me holler."

"How can you possibly see any connection?"

"It's pretty clear. You dump my best man. I'm already short five billets. You're just hoping I'll fall on my ass so you can ride in and take over." Dave stood, face reddening, "Well, you're wrong. Don't expect any sympathy from me. You can take your truth and go fuck yourself with it for all I care. Just leave my people alone." He yanked the door open, banging it against the bunk, and pushed his way into the passage past Seaman Arnold, who was leaning on his broom, shamelessly listening.

"Dave . . ." Mark called through the open door, wanting to have it out with his roommate — convince him *again* that his job was safe — but the other officer was gone. Outside, Arnold bent back to his work. Mark walked slowly to the door, pushed it shut, and flipped the lock. He sat on the bunk as minutes passed.

A knock. "Yes?"

"It's Casso, sir."

Mark opened the door and the petty officer stepped in carrying a bundle of papers. "Need signatures, boss. Yours'll do," he said, placing the pile of personnel actions on the desk. "You all right, sir?"

The note of concern was evident in his voice. Mark responded, "Why do you ask?"

"Oh, it's just that turd, Arnold. Grabbed me in the passageway, said you and Lieutenant Brown had a fight over who should be the engineer."

"Thanks, Jim."

Casso left, pulling the door gently closed.

Mark lay back on the bunk and clamped his eyelids shut. His head felt as if an Alka-Seltzer had been wedged behind his eyes, sizzling and popping in a million tiny explosions. Nausea. Seasick, he told himself. Must be seasick. Always a first time.

✯ Chapter Nine ✯

Mark stayed aboard in Long Beach. He'd seen the city before. It wasn't as bad as the depressing scenery *Modoc* had passed to get there from the naval base — now in the final phases of shut down. Terminal Island wore a constant smoggy coat, like a wad of steel wool spread over the industrial maze. This was one Navy base he didn't care was closing.

He tossed the case file on the desk and tipped his chair back on two legs. He reviewed what he had: a letter and statement from Overmiller, a fruitless search of Lamm's apartment, and a threat from the commanding officer. And that isn't all that's wrong in my wacked-out life. There's Lynn and sneaking out at 0500 so Vicky doesn't spill the beans. Oh yes, mustn't forget Dave Brown, my buddy.

"Well, you've got your health," he said aloud, echoing his mother's rejoinder to any complaint.

He punched the button on his cassette player and Rachmaninoff's Second Piano Concerto began. His own taste ran to Phil Collins and Dolly Parton but Lynn had been encouraging him to broaden his musical experience by giving him several classical tapes. The instrumentals *did* help him think. He closed his eyes and let the music fill him.

★

Captain Bennett had tapped Mark to take the conn again for the pickup in Long Beach. Another opportunity to catch him in a screwup. Well away from the piers, the tow was pulled into position by harbor tugs that jockeyed around the unpowered ship like dogs bringing a stag to ground, nipping here, pushing there, giving a determined shove to pressure its course. Mark relished taking charge of this operation, for here on the ship's bridge he was fully in control — both his training and instincts coming to bear. *Throw me into that briar patch, Bennett. Just watch me.*

The target ship, a survivor of World War II duty guarding merchant ship convoys, had spent forty years mothballed until resurrection — even for service in a new war — had been considered too costly. Now, in Mark's hands, she was being taken to sea for a final time. There was something poetic in the simplicity of what was soon to happen. The target had been stripped of salvageable equipment and hazardous materials at the now-closed Long Beach Naval Shipyard; steam-cleaners had scoured her tanks. She had been ballasted down with water to displace the loss of weight and make her ride easy on the towline.

Clean her up and kill her. Simple, direct, Mark thought, wishing he wouldn't have to return to the mound of legal paperwork on his desk — which was anything but simple and direct.

Mark edged *Modoc* alongside the quiet hulk, standing off fifty yards, then drifting closer. A sailor on the fantail waited for the dead ship's bow to come within range of his throwing arm. On Mark's shouted order, the deck hand held the coiled shot line in one hand and swung the monkey fist — a chunk of lead knotted over with line to the size of a baseball. After a few revolutions of the projectile, the line *whooshed* with the centrifugal force it had built, tugging at the sailor's hand. He let it fly and the monkey fist traced a clean arc across the other ship's bow. A yard worker on the destroyer escort ran forward on the deck to claim the line and haul it across the open space of water. Two others joined him and they pulled increasingly larger lines across the gap from *Modoc* until the hawser, thick as a man's biceps, was made fast.

Modoc moved forward dead slow while Homer Pitkin's deck crew paid out hawser, building a safe separation between the ships. Mark kept his binoculars on the lead tugboat until he was sure the yard workers had climbed aboard and he could see them wave "all clear." The harbor tugs would stay close by, flanking the ship until *Modoc* hauled this piece of floating Navy junk safely out of the harbor. A succession of destroyers and cruisers would *plink* away with their three- and five-inch guns at the hulk. Probably have to send a crew from *Modoc* aboard to scuttle her when the shooting finished.

At five knots, Mark knew the transit south to the operations area off the Coronado Islands would be pure tedium. Porpoises wouldn't even bother playing in the bow wave at this speed. The shoot didn't begin until Monday. That meant almost two days steaming to the operations area and then in circles — squares actually — once they got on station and while they waited for the first of the gunner ships. Mark could use the time between bridge watches to plow through the Lamm case paperwork.

★

Mark had the conn 0400 to 0800 Sunday morning. He preferred the early morning watch so that he could sleep most of the night undisturbed. At 0630 *Modoc* had entered the operations area a hundred miles west of San Diego and away from commercial shipping lanes. At 0730 he called to the bo'sun mate of the watch, "Pass muster on station."

The bo'sun raised his pipe to the 1MC microphone and blew attention. The two-note call faded across the morning sea. "Now all hands muster on station. Departments report to the bridge."

In a few minutes messengers began arriving at the pilothouse with slips of paper reporting all present or accounted for.

"Sir?" Mark turned, lowering his binoculars. It was the quartermaster who served as navigator and record keeper. "Sir, engineering is missing one man."

"Which one?"

"Didn't say, sir. They're checking berthing now."

Mark ran the procedure for *man-overboard* through his mind and knew it would be impossible to make a quick turn with the hulk in tow to circle back to a man in the water. Wouldn't matter anyway now. That maneuver worked only if someone saw the sailor hit the water and reported to the bridge immediately.

He checked the course they'd covered on the plotting board. A straight line to the op area. No contacts during the night except with an oil tanker beating north. Mark peered at the radarscope's glowing display and clicked the range knob to maximum. Nothing of size. No help should they need it quickly. Probably wouldn't need it, he thought, some sailor stayed up late reading skin magazines and overslept was all it would turn out to be.

Happened a million times before, but I'd better get ready, just in case.

Anticipate. Anticipation, ceaseless drilling, had kept him out of trouble on the bridge and in the engine rooms so far and it made the watches go faster. Fantasy disasters, rote responses.

He stepped to the starboard wing. The seas would not be helpful, he thought, gazing toward the eastern horizon. A light chop confused the surface and would obscure a man in the water. Until the sun crawled higher, glare would be another problem. Cold waters at this latitude would quickly bring on hypothermia and it was unlikely that a man over the side would be wearing a life jacket.

"Engineering can't find him, sir."

"Get his name," Mark ordered. Maybe, just maybe, it's a mistake.

"Overmiller," the quartermaster said after a brief exchange on the phone.

"Oh, shit."

Mark took the phone receiver and dialed one, zero. "Captain, this is the OOD. One man missing at muster and a search hasn't turned him up. No reports of a man overboard. Checking, sir. Still checking." Without waiting for a response, he tapped the phone hook and dialed again.

"Lieutenant Brown? Any luck with the search? I've notified the CO. When is the last time anyone saw him? Okay, keep me informed. Skipper should be on the bridge in a couple of minutes."

He turned to the quartermaster. "Work out a plot to bring us to a reverse course in the shortest time. Remember the tow at fifteen hundred yards." Urgency might save a life, if he could determine where to look — what two-foot spot in a vast sea?

"Aye aye, sir." The man bent over his chart.

"It's Lieutenant Brown, for the OOD." The bo'sun held the phone at arm's length.

"Go ahead, Dave."

"Nobody's seen Overmiller since around 2100 last night. The other departments are checking their spaces, too."

"Have you got your biggest goof-offs in on the search? They know all the hiding places."

"First ones I sent out. I'd have sent Overmiller if he wasn't the one missing."

"Brief me!" Captain Bennett stormed onto the bridge.

"CO is on the bridge," the bo'sun called out.

Mark replaced the receiver. "Captain, Fireman Apprentice Overmiller missed muster. Nobody's seen him since 2100 and a search of the ship hasn't turned him up." Over the captain's shoulder he could see the quartermaster flash fingers in the air and move his lips silently, reporting his plot to reverse course. Mark verbalized the quartermaster's message: "And to make a turn back to the reverse bearing will take fifty minutes unless we abandon the tow. Make it a navigation hazard. If he's in the water, he might have been there for eleven hours already. Would take almost twelve more to backtrack. Of course, there are currents that would have moved him off the reverse line. No other large contacts in the area."

Bennett answered quickly. "Make the turn with your tow, station lookouts and notify SURFPAC. Tell them we may be late for rendezvous tomorrow morning. Request help from any ships that may come into the area. I'll be in my cabin. I want reports every half-hour," Bennett said without emotion, and left the bridge.

"I'm ready to relieve you, sir." Chief Fenton stepped forward from a corner where he'd been watching.

"Very well, Chief, I'll turn over the conn and continue with what I've started. It'll take two of us." Mark checked the quartermaster's plot. "Helm, come right five degrees rudder and steady up on course two-eight-five."

"Aye aye, sir."

Mark briefed Chief Fenton. The two men stepped apart and faced each other. Fenton saluted. "I relieve you, sir."

"I stand relieved." Mark returned the salute and grabbed the high-frequency radio handset to make the SURFPAC notification. "Muskrat, Muskrat, this is Bojangles, Bojangles . . ."

★

Captain Bennett stood near the small table in his cabin toying with a pawn, tapping it softly against the alabaster chessboard. Mark remained stiff, standing near the door, silently waiting for some word.

"I don't like this at all," the captain finally said, "Just too damned convenient."

"We've covered our tracks. No sign of him anywhere. Currents probably took him miles away. Every space on the ship has been double-checked, even the fuel tanks and voids. Unless he simply flew away in the night, he went overboard. None of the other ships in the area have found anything, either.

"It's been almost twenty-four hours. Shall I send the message: *Missing, presumed dead,* and ask for further instructions? His parents live in Kansas. SURFPAC can arrange for a casualty assistance calls officer from the area."

"This doesn't get you off the hook, Mister Palmer."

"Hook, sir?"

"The Lamm case, goddamnit."

Mark realized they'd been having two different conversations. "Hadn't thought about that," he replied in an even tone. Then, "We lost a man at sea, *sir*, or doesn't that matter?" He immediately wished he hadn't challenged Bennett.

The answer came back in unexpectedly quiet words. "If he fell over, why didn't the fantail watch see him or hear splashing or calling?"

"It was dark. Overmiller could have been unconscious. There are any number of reasons, and the water is cold."

"He was bound and gagged, maybe weighted. Murder, Mister Palmer, murder."

"Murder?"

"I'd say we have a prime suspect," the captain continued. "Your boy Lamm."

"I'll certainly explore that possibility, but I don't think it's likely. Lamm is not the type. Murder is a little extreme. Besides, how could we prove it without a body or witnesses?"

"Have you already eliminated the possibility of witnesses?"

"No, sir. But someone would have come forward by now if they had seen anything."

"You sound pretty sure about that. Could be inconvenient for you, couldn't it?"

"Captain, I protest, and I'll do it in writing to SURFPAC if I have to. You have no cause to talk to me like this, as if I had something to do with losing Overmiller."

"And you think SURFPAC will believe you, an admitted liar? You really amuse me. You're not in a position to protest or bargain or dictate to me. You *are* in a position to carry out my orders or face dereliction charges before a court-martial."

The captain was right. Mark knew that once the Navy selected an officer for command at sea it took a great deal to unseat him. Even in wartime it took extraordinary measures to have him officially relieved — practically an act of Congress. Strange, he thought, captains lose their commands for reasons other than the way they treat their men. Groundings, collisions, poor seamanship seemed to be the only justifiable reasons for relief.

"I'll start the investigation right away, sir." Mark knew when to back down. Now is good, he thought, *before* would have been better. He turned to the door.

"Mark."

"Yes, sir?" he said, facing the captain.

"Dismissed."

✯ Chapter Ten ✯

Mark returned to the bridge to review the ship's log, taking navigation data for his narrative report of Overmiller's loss. What he wrote would be transmitted electronically to SURFPAC, setting in motion notification of Overmiller's family and perhaps an outside investigation. He'd conduct his own inquiry on board now the coordinated 32-hour search had been ended. Ships in the area would continue to keep watch but the formal search was over. Only luck could have located Overmiller under these circumstances. Too much time had passed before he'd been noticed missing.

✯

Occasional thunder of five-inch guns and shells exploding on target penetrated the steel wall of Mark's stateroom. A lumbering supply ship followed the combatants with her twenty-millimeter machine guns chattering, passing close abeam on the reverse course. Stupid exercise, he thought, remembering the gunnery exercise manual and its diagrams. The best practice for a ship like the one passing, or for *Modoc* in this missile warfare age, would be running for cover or disappearing entirely. The auxiliary ships fired their guns more for the morale of the crew than any actual consideration of defense. Mark had wanted to watch the shoot; instead, Petty Officer Third Class Monty Pincus now sat alongside Mark's desk. The temperature in the stateroom had climbed with each of the forty-eight men who had entered so far and responded that they hadn't seen anything happen to Overmiller. The air conditioning had been working sporadically all day and there were almost forty more interviews to go. Wait until Dave racks out tonight in this sauna, Mark thought; he'll get it fixed. In a perverse way, Mark welcomed his current discomfort, like the effort of physical exercise — something to endure and overcome.

Mark watched the eyes of each man he questioned for a glimmer, a twitch, any gesture that would indicate a lie. He saw nervousness but he expected that. He found himself wanting to find an eyewitness — two or three would be better — with an irrefutable account of Overmiller's loss.

Pincus spoke. "Yes, sir, I knew Randy, we were both from Kansas y'know so we had something in common — sometimes hit the beach together, go drinkin' — the regular stuff. Him bein' dead and all is a shock. I know he didn't get along with lots of people, especially senior people, but he was a good guy, y'know. Funny too. He'd do a Michael Jackson impression, singing 'I'm bad, I'm bad . . .' dancing like he does, moonwalking. Mostly when he was drinkin'. Tried gettin' in karaoke bars, but he couldn't pass for twenty-one."

"Tell me what you know about the circumstances of his death," Mark said, hoping that he'd finally found someone who would talk — someone who thought the missing sailor was worth caring about.

"Don't know nothing about that, Lieutenant. We

bunked in different compartments so I didn't even know he was missing 'til the word was passed after muster."

Another dead-end. If anyone had seen Overmiller fall or jump and hadn't raised the alarm, he'd be foolish to admit it a day and a half later. He'd be up on charges himself, face prison. Every hour that passed made it less likely Mark would ever get the real story. One possibility remained — a confession — but who? Who should he ask, who should he pressure?

If he found no witnesses to murder and no one confessed, he'd be facing Bennett, who would see him as failing to carry out orders, a derelict officer, or worse, one working at cross purposes to the commanding officer. He wished momentarily he *could* unearth a murder.

He had Lamm sent in last.

"I take it you suspect me of throwing Overmiller to the fish, Lieutenant," he said.

Mark suddenly saw the similarities of their positions. He wouldn't, however, allow Lamm to be insubordinate, whatever the reason.

"Will you talk to me about this?"

"All right, sir. No lawyers out here."

"You don't have to talk just because we're at sea."

"It's okay. Feel like I'm going to get fucked no matter what I do."

"Petty Officer Lamm," Mark said softly, "you're a good sailor and you haven't been convicted of anything . . ."

"Yet."

Mark's voice took on a new stridency. "I'm trying to tell you I understand the strain you're under, but you'd be better off keeping your mouth shut if you're going to start insulting officers. I'll ignore it once, but if you want to screw yourself, I'll let you."

He locked Lamm with a penetrating stare for a few seconds, then handed him a rights sheet. Mark turned back to the papers on the desk. He'd give Lamm a minute to calm down, adjust his attitude — and calm down himself.

"Sorry, Lieutenant, you're right." Lamm signaled the end of his contemplation and handed back the rights sheet, lines initialed and signed. He'd talk. Mark entered the time and date on the form and signed it himself.

"The reason I gave you your rights . . . do you understand them?"

"Yes, sir."

"The reason is not necessarily that you are a suspect in the loss of Overmiller, but other action is pending and I can't talk to you about anything that might be remotely connected. At the moment I have no evidence a crime has been committed." He studied Lamm's face, detecting a slight softening of tension around the eyes.

Mark started the tape recorder. "Did you see Overmiller during Saturday night?"

"Only at chow. He's been staying clear of me. Lieutenant Brown took him out of my division. The other guys have to pick up the slack. Think he's staying clear of them, too. He runs around with a third class from Operations Division. Seen them in town together."

"Pincus?"

"Yeah."

"Did anyone have a grudge against Overmiller?"

Lamm laughed. "You mean besides me? Sure. Plenty of people. He could be a real pain in the ass. Everyone else got stuck doing his work, standing his watches, even when he was still in the division. He spent half his time in sick bay trying to convince the corpsman he was suffering from something or other."

"Anybody in particular have it in for him, make threats?"

"Wish I could say yes, but no, none I was aware of. They just blew him off as another mama's boy."

"Anything you can add that might shed light on what could have happened to him?"

"No, sir, nothing."

End of the line, Mark thought. That perverse little *kamikaze* — Overmiller probably threw himself overboard just to stir up trouble.

He pushed the stop button. "Any ideas, theories, about what might have happened?"

Lamm eyed the tape machine, then raised his gaze to Mark's face. His voice dropped, barely above a whisper, as if to deny anyone who might be outside the thin sheet-metal stateroom door an opportunity to hear. "When we're at sea, some of the younger guys sneak out on deck at night and sit near the rail, smoke marijuana. I've tried catching 'em before, but they throw everything over the side soon's anyone gets close. All I can do then is let them know I'll be watching. Maybe deprive them of some dope."

Mark was surprised. Not because men were smoking marijuana, but because Lamm had tried to do something about it. Too many of the senior petty officers and junior officers looked the other way. The smoking went on even when the sailors knew they might be identified in a random urine test.

"How could they be on deck and not be seen by the OOD or the other officers?"

"They'd get between the boat davits and under the

lifeboat hull. Could only see them from directly at sea or from under the lifeboat. There's a small ledge there and the lifelines don't cross outboard of the boat. Easy to fall out of there, especially someone high on pot."

"That's the most reasonable thing I've heard all day. Thanks for sharing that, Petty Officer Lamm. Oh, one other thing, you ever catch Overmiller under the boats?"

"No, sir, but I had put out word in my division that I knew about people going out there to smoke and I'd be watching. I wanted to catch someone just going under the boat, when they couldn't throw the stuff overboard."

"And you would have grabbed them and taken the marijuana out of their pockets?"

"Yes, sir."

"And violated their rights with an illegal search and seizure." Mark held up a hand to stop Lamm from protesting. "Before you say what I know you want to say, I think you should listen. I've heard it all before and I agree, it stinks, but being a senior petty officer makes you the 'authorities.' Puts you in the same category as shore patrol or base police or even NIS."

"I didn't realize that. Thought I could do some good."

"Maybe you could have, but chances are that one of the dope smokers would have brought charges against you."

"All I wanted was to get them to stop smoking that stuff on the ship. It's too damned dangerous."

"Don't think I don't support the idea — it's just the method that won't do. We probably could have gotten them with a stepped up schedule of urine tests — all nice and legal."

The two men sat quietly for what seemed to be hours. Mark was unsure what to say next. Because the revelation of the marijuana that might explain how Overmiller had been lost had been a result of his talk with Lamm, doubt was cast on the truth of the story which conveniently exonerated the petty officer. That it would also serve as a motive for Overmiller's accusing letter was something Mark didn't want to consider at the moment. Lamm had to know he was a prime suspect if the disappearance turned out to be murder. There was little chance Mark would find any proof of that, but he needed more to clear Lamm entirely. Someone else must know about the hide-away, or that Overmiller was doing drugs. He couldn't go to the captain with less and expect him to believe Lamm had nothing to do with the missing man. He wondered what he could say to the captain. What will he believe?

"Anyone else know about the smoking under the lifeboats?"

"I told Casso."

"When?"

"Probably three months back. He said he'd keep a lookout when he could."

★

"Captain," Mark said, standing before the desk, holding the document he had secretly prepared, "if you will sign this authorization for a health and comfort inspection of engineering berthing spaces, I think I'll be able to unearth some evidence in the Overmiller case." He laid the sheet on the desk blotter.

"What do you expect to find?" Bennett asked as he pointedly drew his hand away from the pen that lay near it on the desk. "We could use a search warrant."

"Skipper, to be quite frank, I'm on a fishing trip and this is the only legal way to catch anything. I only have suspicions, not enough for a search warrant."

Bennett grinned. "Finally decided to stop playing

around with this thing, huh? What made you stop looking for some 'legal' reason to sit on your ass and do nothing?"

"We lost a man at sea and we owe it to ourselves and his parents to find out what happened."

"I see, if you figure the cause has a noble objective you're willing to do your job. What would convince you to work for less heroic ends?" Bennett leaned back, obviously satisfied with his point.

"Your signature on the authorization, sir," Mark said, locking eyes with the captain. "And the order to empty Overmiller's locker."

Bennett's jaw muscles tightened, making it clear he did not like being included in Mark's plans for this dirty, intrusive job. Yet, he had little choice.

"Well, we haven't had a health and comfort inspection in quite a while. Probably time for it anyway." Bennett signed the authorization and the order to clear Overmiller's locker and inventory his personal effects that had been on his desk since morning. He let the papers lie in front of him. Mark stepped forward and snatched them.

"Thank you, sir."

"Mark," said the captain in an easy tone, "sometime when this is all over, I think we should have a talk. Straighten a few things out. Hate to see a good officer — and that's what I think you are — I hate to see a good officer run astray."

Bennett's latest turnabout left Mark unimpressed — if anything, more suspicious and distrustful. He's jerking me off, Mark thought, trying to put out some imagined brushfire. He played his guessing game for a half-second longer, then smiled and said, "I'd like that a lot, sir," hoping he had tinged his words with only enough insincerity to make Bennett wonder.

Modoc's boat deck ended sixty feet forward of the rounded stern and overlooked the ship's broad fantail. A pair of thirty-foot open boats for salvage and rescue work were positioned there along with two lifeboats. Below, on the fantail, a few men were taking down layers of thick hawser in elongated figure eights — like a handwriting exercise — so it would pay out smoothly without kinking. The watch sat near the towing hawser on a stubby steel bitt the size of a fire hydrant. His job was to watch the ride of the towed ship and monitor tension on the line. A boring watch, especially in the pitch black of night. A man could easily doze off for a few minutes and miss anything that happened around him — even a man overboard.

Mark walked to the starboard lifeboat station where the motor whaleboat, packed with emergency provisions, hung from a pair of tall, curved davits like a trout caught head and tail by two fishermen.

He crawled under the boat to the small ledge where he found a few black, lightly charred spots in the paint. The haze gray color had mostly faded and oxidized from the weather, but in some spots was clean of oxidation and salt buildup. No question, men had been here, hidden, probably smoking marijuana. He looked over the side.

A platform for salvage work jutted from the ship's side. A man falling from the deck above, nearly twenty feet, would crash into the platform before rolling into the water. It would make sense that the watch hadn't heard screams if Overmiller had hit his head and been unconscious when he entered the water. Now all he had to do was find a witness who had seen Overmiller use this hideout. He was sure he'd find drugs of some kind when he emptied the dead sailor's locker.

★

"What kind of shit are you pulling now?" Dave Brown said, scowling, jutting his jaw.

"Read the order. Health and comfort inspection. I need one other officer to help — you or your assistant. I'm going down to berthing now. Send the divisions one at a time starting in ten minutes."

"And who's supposed to run the plant while you're playing games?"

"You'll just have to spread them out to cover all the jobs. You've done it before."

"Why are you singling engineering out for this hassle? Gettin' itchy to take over?"

"Dave, I'd really like to talk to you about this when we both have more time. You don't have to worry about that."

"Who are you trying to con? I hear about you going in for long chats with Bennett. Gettin' cozy, ready to slip it to me when I'm not looking — a little billet rotation."

Dave stalked away, shouting for Ensign Gordon Mackey above the clatter of the engine room. Mark climbed the ladder to the main deck, walked forward and down another ladder into the berthing spaces. The smell was the same as that of every other ship's berthing he'd been in. Twenty year's worth of sweaty bodies living in a locker room. *The senses adjust,* he told himself as he dialed Casso. He needed the petty officer to watch the forward berthing door to be sure nobody sneaked in to empty a locker of contraband while they were conducting inspections in another section.

The enlisted man is wily and bears constant watching. He

couldn't remember where he'd heard that. He had laughed over it with Tom LaCroix, who had also been a white-hat sailor before commissioning. Now he felt an embarrassment in his apparent heed of the old saw. *Just commonsense security measures,* he told himself, *while I rifle the personal belongings of forty people.* Allegedly, a search for items that would jeopardize the health and comfort of the crew: food items that would attract bugs, nonregulation flammable materials, clothing that hadn't seen soap and water in months. That's what it was supposed to be. Of course, anything of an illegal nature that happened to turn up would be confiscated and a report chit written.

There was no secret about what a health and comfort inspection was. That's why they were kept secret until the men were called away from their jobs to stand around while gentlemen from the officer corps pawed through the one bit of privacy the enlisted man had — his locker.

☆ Chapter Eleven ☆

In a clearing he had made on his desk amid the mounting stack of papers, Mark stacked a pyramid of three plastic thirty-five millimeter film cans. Without looking he placed them in a line, moved the one on the left to the right end and pushed the other two forward. He repeated the move, then stacked them again as anyone might idly play with three coins. The gesture, under other circumstances, would have meant no more than peeling the label off a beer bottle or drawing designs in the water condensed on the bar.

To twenty-three-year-old Boiler Tender Third Class Virgil Morris, Mark's fingerplay meant more. He was keeping the slightly built sailor's attention on the three cans and his mind focused on what was in them. Pot and rolling papers.

He knows the rules, Mark said to himself. I know the rules too, and they don't say anything about a trick like keeping the evidence in sight during questioning. He almost wished the instructors in legal school hadn't been so charmingly helpful with their mind games. With the cans as a constant reminder that he'd been caught red-handed with marijuana aboard ship, in all likelihood

Morris would cough up a confession, making any further investigation of him unnecessary. Captain's mast that day would be the formality where Bennett could play whatever role he wished — indignant that anyone would do wrong on his ship, or the beleaguered captain-father of misguided souls.

In dramatic exasperation he would inquire, "Do you want me to call your mother and tell her what you've done?" Then he would announce that, though he regretted doing it, he would have to take one stripe and half a month's pay for two months, assign two hours of extra duty a day during sixty days restriction to the ship. The maximum. He could make them cry with repentance.

Morris's eyes barely contained the wetness that threatened to gush down his face. His voice cracked, but he would not ask for water to stop the choking squeak of his words. Mark had trouble working up the appropriate outrage he knew he ought to feel over his discovery in Morris's locker. For years this amount of pot had been a misdemeanor on the streets of California. Even after voters had approved an initiative to allow medical marijuana for the terminally ill, politicians wrangled over the question and police still busted dying cancer patients. No ambiguity about it in the Navy, though. Possession was a crime that would cost Petty Officer Morris dearly. Cash alone came to nearly thirteen hundred dollars from his pay.

"Okay, so you admit to smoking this garbage between the boat davits. You ever smoke with Overmiller?"

Morris lowered his chin until it nearly touched his chest.

"You might as well know I found Overmiller's stash when I inventoried his locker. The way I see it you potheads stick together, making me wonder what you had to do with Overmiller going overboard."

Morris jerked his head up, the movement spilling tears down his cheeks. "I didn't have nothing to do with that," he croaked.

Mark spoke calmly. "I figure you and Overmiller were sitting out there getting stoned and he picked a fight with you over the price of a joint or whatever you dopers argue about. You got pissed and threw him over the side. Wouldn't take much, a little shove. Simple. Clean. Man overboard in the middle of the night and nobody the wiser."

"No, sir, *no,* sir . . ." Morris was crying openly now, his mouth drawn into an ugly rectangle. "It wasn't me, sir . . . I swear it wasn't me."

"Well who could it have been if it wasn't you? I didn't find pot in anyone else's locker. Just yours and Overmiller's. Cozy, you two."

Mark wanted to gag. Morris was nothing more than a stunned fly and he was pulling his wings off one at a time, keeping him off balance, making him spin tighter and tighter in circles as he frantically buzzed to free himself. Except Mark would never do this to a fly.

"Arnold, it was Arnold went out with him Saturday." Morris named the sailor who haunted the passageway outside the officers' staterooms, holding a broom or swab, looking busy. Listening.

"You're going to have to convince me of that. You're going to make me want to believe you, Morris. And you better be right. False accusations are prima facie — the best evidence, because you've written them down and signed them." Mark shoved a statement blank across the desk and let his hand fall back on the three plastic film cans.

"You write the whole thing here about smoking marijuana, about Overmiller and Arnold, or whoever you decide to try and hang this thing on. But it better be good or that's your own conviction."

Mark snapped the tape recorder off, knowing he'd be wise to erase the tape once Morris committed his story to paper. The man looked smaller now as he bent over the paper. His hand shook and he wiped back the tears with his dungaree shirtsleeve. Mark looked at the iron-on patch on Morris's sleeve, a third class crow — a chevron with a spread eagle above it. Morris could kiss that good-bye.

Mark watched him write for a while, then turned to prepare a search warrant. If Morris feels miserable now, wait until he goes to mast, Mark thought. He'd heard it said the punishment part is the easiest because there's a certainty about it. Pay so much, serve so many days, scrub so many decks. It is waiting for the sentence to be announced that rips a man's guts. Mark knew one thing for sure; anything less than the full load of punishment was rare, and there had to be powerfully extenuating circumstances to convince Bennett to reduce the penalty.

★

Mark laid the search warrant on the captain's desk while keeping the folder with Morris's statement tucked under his arm. Bennett studied the paper, then looked up.

"Arnold, huh? Not surprised, way he hovers around. How does he figure into this?"

"I'm pretty sure he either witnessed or had something to do with Overmiller's death."

"And you figure to sweat him with this?"

"Yes, sir." The old man had seen too many cops-and-robbers movies. *Sweat him* — straight out of *Kojak* reruns. But that was exactly what Mark planned to do.

"You have a witness that Arnold has this stuff?"

"Yes sir. Casso is keeping him on ice in my stateroom so he doesn't let the cat out of the bag," Mark responded with his own cop jargon. "It's Morris. You'll be seeing him at mast for marijuana he had in his locker."

Bennett grinned, "Once you get your feet wet, you take off like a ball of fire," he said, mixing his own trite metaphors.

★

Seaman Arnold stood in the berthing compartment between the bunks first looking sullen then indignant. "Shee-it, man. Why you think I got somethin' in there? Someone's tellin' you lies and you're believin' 'em."

Casso stood closer to the sailor, ready to restrain him if necessary, while Mark riffled the pages of paperbacks he found stacked neatly in one corner of the locker. Something made him concentrate on Camus's *The Stranger,* out of place among the westerns and spy thrillers spread out on the bunk. A pair of thin sheets of paper fell to the blanket from between the pages.

Mark used his ballpoint to flip them over. Each white sheet had a dragon lightly imprinted in gray. A hundred tiny black stars in even rows covered the three-inch square. A third of the stars from one sheet had been removed, cut neatly with scissors.

Mark had never seen blotter acid, but he remembered from his drug reference book that each star marked the location of an invisible drop of dried LSD. One star on the tongue and the doper wouldn't know where he was — or care. He carefully pushed the sheets back between the pages, avoiding skin contact; the drug could be absorbed through the pores.

There was enough here to send the whole crew on a trip. The powerful hallucinogen had recently regained its popularity after years of declining use, probably because it was so easy to smuggle and hide.

"Doesn't look like anybody's been lying about you, Arnold. How much more of this garbage you got? I don't think even you are stupid enough to keep it all in one spot."

"You'll never find it, sucker." Arnold took a step back and Casso clamped a fist around the sailor's arm. "You fuckin' zeros! You gonna pay!" Arnold screamed. "Get your fuckin' hands offa me, you slimy shit."

Casso grabbed Arnold's other arm and shoved him against a bunk.

"Your ass is goin' on a trip, fucker," Arnold spat. "You zeros gotta drink somethin' sometime. I'll fix you some Kool-Aid when you ain't lookin'."

Mark's anger welled. His urge to swing his fist into the punk's face — to crack bones, to see blood — had to be controlled. He turned away from the defiant face of the seaman.

Arnold breathed hard, trying to break Casso's grip but was outweighed and firmly pinned. Mark laid the book aside and continued searching. He knew from Morris's statement where to find the plastic baggies of marijuana rolled in a pair of socks and the miniature pipe for smoking it secreted under a ledge at the front of the locker. Made from tiny hydraulic parts, the pipe might have passed as a piece of engine room junk, except for the burned residue at the edge of the bowl. That would test out as marijuana ash, no doubt. Couldn't be anything else except maybe hashish.

When Arnold's rage subsided, Casso and the corpsman managed to get a urine sample that would show whether he had used marijuana within the past two weeks. The corpsman used his field test kit and found a positive reading. Mark had Arnold cold.

★

Later, Mark sat in one of the vinyl-covered chairs opposite the captain, both of them listening to a small cassette player that poured out Arnold's confession and the details of what had happened Saturday. The sailor had been willing to talk when Mark mentioned the charge might be murder.

". . . was really gettin' high and I tol' him to shut up or someone would hear us. That fuckin' Lamm was always pokin' aroun'. He wouldn't quit talkin' and I tol' him I was gonna leave. He shut up for a while . . ."

Bennett leaned closer to the machine, a smile playing on his lips. The batteries were beginning to die, and Arnold's voice sounded progressively deeper as the man told his story through a throat constricted with fear and defiance.

". . . so I went back to my rack and went to sleep. I wasn't feeling too good. Overmiller was havin' a bad trip; he ain't had acid before. Spose I shoulda' stayed with him, that dumb shit. Goin' on about his old man not givin' a fuck and his mom, cryin' about not having money."

The tape ended and Bennett leaned back, creaking the chair. "So what do you recommend on this one, Mark?" He spoke through a grin.

"Don't see any choice for Arnold but a court-martial for drug possession and distribution. Nobody actually saw Overmiller fall, but I scraped this off the sponson below the davits." He held up a small plastic bag with scrapings of dried blood mixed with flakes of gray paint. "Think it will prove out to be Overmiller's and would explain why nobody heard him go over if he hit his head and was unconscious — or dead."

Bennett examined the bag as though he could divine the chemical makeup of its contents with his eyes. Mark could see he was momentarily satisfied, yet still disappointed Lamm was not apparently involved.

"I'll write up the investigation and preliminary conclusions on the Overmiller case for SURFPAC. We have enough to declare Arnold a danger to the crew. He threatened to poison the wardroom water supply with LSD."

Bennett jerked forward in his chair. "I thought you said you found the LSD in a book!"

"I did. But that doesn't mean there isn't more stashed somewhere that we'd never find in a year of searching. Was probably dealing the stuff. No way of knowing, though. I got him under guard in the chain locker until we can offload him to the brig. They'll hold him until trial."

The captain relaxed. Smiled. "Four-oh job, Mark. Do as well on the Lamm case and I'll see to it a letter of commendation goes into your service record for this one."

And another medal at quarters? Mark thought bitterly. "About Lamm. I still don't have much to go with — even for an admin board."

"I know you'll find something, Mark." Bennett's smile was gone.

"It's beginning to look a lot like Lamm was set up —"

Bennett's fist on the desk stopped him. "Are you starting that shit again?" Bennett was on his feet. "I'm getting just plain sick and tired of your insubordination."

Mark stood. "Is it an order then? Do you order me to go ahead with the board on Lamm?"

"You bet your ass, mister!"

"Aye aye, sir. Request permission to leave."

★

Except for bridge watches and meals, Mark spent the rest of the extended sea period in his stateroom preparing the Arnold and Morris cases. Their one-week schedule had become two with the disruption caused by Overmiller's loss. Dave stayed away during the day and their forced meetings at night in their shared room were perfunctory. Just as well, Mark thought. He didn't want to spend time arguing when he needed every minute for the mass of legal paperwork that had spilled from his desk to his bunk.

Bennett, as if equally hesitant about another scene, had stopped calling. Casso slipped in and out delivering smooth drafts, picking up roughs, without saying more than a word or two each time.

On Friday, the day before *Modoc* returned to San Diego, Mark realized he hadn't thought about Lynn and Vicky during the entire two weeks. Now he was eager to see them both, but especially Lynn, to feel the warmth of her arms. He tried not to think about Tony.

"I probably ought to just give it all up. Forget Lynn. Resign my commission, move to Hawaii and make puka shell necklaces," he said into the empty stateroom before falling, exhausted, into his bunk. The alarm was set for 0315. The morning watch. He'd be bringing *Modoc* into San Diego and needed his rest. Bennett would be watching him again, ready to pounce.

✯ Chapter Twelve ✯

A PAIR OF BRIG CHASERS wearing Shore Patrol brassards and carrying .45–caliber semiautomatic pistols in holsters leaned against a van on the pier, waiting for Arnold. Mark guided *Modoc* to a gentle stop against the mole. The usual gathering of wives milled about in a loose group waiting to greet their husbands. So unlike the enthusiastic crowds meeting the aircraft carriers home-ported at North Island Naval Air Station across the bay at the tip of Coronado. Returning from six-month and longer deployments to world hot spots — Iraq, Somalia, and now Kosovo — the flat tops were met by cheering, waving wives and children in the thousands. Among them, a military band, banners, hand-painted welcome signs and TV crews to record the happy reunions and interview the captain and admiral.

Modoc slips in and out of port like a pickpocket, Mark thought.

With the brow in place, creating a walkway linking ship and pier, Casso escorted Arnold to the van while Mark watched from the bridge. The two policemen shoved Arnold against the truck, patted him down, and snapped handcuffs around his wrists. When Arnold protested, they pushed him roughly through the barred rear doors of the van. One brig chaser took the form from Casso, inspected it briefly, then signed, taking a copy. Another consignment of meat.

Mark gazed up at the blue-painted sweep of the San Diego-Coronado Bay Bridge, curving, descending to the sparkling green splotch of Coronado. He drew a deep breath through his nose and picked up the ever-present Navy scent of diesel exhaust. Sight of the Bay Bridge inexplicably filled him with a longing to travel, to see more of his own country.

The day had dawned diamondlike in the clarity of the air and Point Loma stood out in sharp detail beyond the bridge. A good day for a ride with the top down, he thought, Lynn next to him and Vicky in the tiny backseat where he could sneak his hand back and tickle her knees.

Mark ordered *shift colors* and the Stars and Stripes were raised on the jackstaff at the stern. The in-port officer of the day took over the watch on the quarterdeck, freeing Mark to go below to his stateroom.

He gathered his laundry, stuffing the clothes into a mesh bag. Then he secured the growing volume of paperwork and interview tapes from the Lamm and Overmiller cases in his safe, spinning the dial as the phone jangled. He hesitated a moment before deciding to grab it. "Lieutenant Palmer."

"Lieutenant Palmer? This is Captain Bennett."

"Captain?" Now what's going on, Mark wondered. Bennett sounds positively polite.

"Perhaps you could join me in my cabin for a moment before you leave."

Out of character, Mark thought, as he tapped lightly on the captain's door.

With the captain was a woman wearing a cream colored skirt and jacket. Her auburn hair fell in a gentle curve to her shoulders. Early forties, Mark guessed — slim and well groomed.

"Mark, may I present Mrs. Overmiller. She flew out from Liberal, Kansas," Bennett said.

Mark reached for her hand. "I'm sorry about the loss of your son, Mrs. Overmiller."

"Yes. Thank you." They each took a chair.

"Mrs. Overmiller's already had a visit with the base chaplain yesterday but he really didn't know much. Since you are investigating, I thought you could fill in some details." Bennett, clearly taken with her, spoke with a nervous timbre.

"Well, at this point there isn't much information. I'll turn what I have over to the admiral's staff to complete the official report. It'll be sent to you. With Captain Bennett's permission . . ." The skipper nodded. "I can tell you what I think happened. The ship was steaming at night. Randy was apparently sitting on the deck edge near the lifeboat and fell. He wasn't noticed missing until morning — it could have been as long as eight hours. Other ships joined the search but we couldn't find him."

Mrs. Overmiller absorbed this information without reaction. "Did it have anything to do with drugs?"

Mark glanced at Bennett, who quickly glanced away. "Yes, ma'am, it's possible. One man admitted to using LSD earlier that same evening with your son. He's awaiting court-martial on drug charges."

"My husband and I were afraid of that. We thought Randy had beaten his drug problem — that the Navy would keep him straightened out. I guess not."

"Excuse me," Bennett entered the conversation, "did Mr. Overmiller fly out with you?"

"No. He had business," she paused, gathering

composure. "I should be truthful... he said that if the Navy couldn't find Randy, we wouldn't be able to either but . . . he had given up on our son some time ago." She paused again, clearly uncomfortable.

"Mrs. Overmiller, may I ask you a question," Mark intervened. "Did Randy ever mention a petty officer named Lamm in letters or maybe in a phone call?"

"Lamm? I don't recall hearing him say that name but we didn't hear from him very often. Randy never sent letters . . . he was dyslexic, you know, and had a hard time writing — embarrassed about it." She extended her hand to Mark. "If you can help me call a taxi, I'll be going. You must have your own families waiting for you."

Bennett rose and stepped around the desk. "I'd be honored to take you to your hotel. My car is just outside on the pier."

★

With his bag of dirty uniforms slung over his shoulder, Mark walked almost a mile to the lot where he had left the Fiat. The Spyder always looked forlorn sitting there — orange paint covered with dust and a fine black haze of soot from the exhaust stacks of nearby ships, all splotched with water drops. The old car — he jokingly called it a classic — was filthy but safe. He would have to invest in a canvas cover for it, he thought for the hundredth time as he turned the key in the ignition and listened to the immediate catch of the engine. He patted the dashboard, smiling. The one thing I can count on, sometimes.

★

He opened the sliding glass door and the other two windows in his apartment. He kept the apartment clean, almost sterile, and never noticed the starkness of the pictureless walls except when he returned from sea. Cora took all the pictures. Furniture, too. Everything. Mark preferred it that way, used to say he didn't want anything that wouldn't fit into his car, as if he were apt to light out for Alaska immediately. Only he never had.

He dialed Lynn's number. She picked up on the first ring. "Hi, honey. I'm back from the forefront of freedom," he said into the receiver. "We've held off the terrorists for another week."

"Oh, Mark."

"What's wrong, Lynn?" He detected trouble in her voice.

"Nothing."

"Come on, that's my line. Look, I'll be right over. Just gotta change clothes."

"No, Mark. Don't come. Not right now," she said, sounding empty, as if she had cried herself dry.

"What is it? Is Vicky all right?"

"She's with Tony. *She's* all right."

"Then what?" He felt an invisible hand clutch his heart and squeeze, the same one that comes with a telephone ringing at 3:00 A.M. Lynn had never been this distant. When she didn't answer he continued, "Look, if I can't come there, meet me. I've got to talk to you." He glanced at his watch. "Meet me in a half-hour at the mall near the escalator. Will you do that?"

"All right."

"Lynn, whatever it is, I'll help. We can —"

"All right!" she screamed. "I said all right!" She slammed the phone down.

★

Mark found an empty bench near the mall escalator and waited. Like the Israelis and Arabs meeting at Camp

David — neutral ground. He'd control his urge to lash out at Lynn until he found out what was behind her anger. Ten-thirty came. He had by then discerned the rhythm of squeaks and knocks emanating from the escalator to his left. A piece of pink gum squashed between the treads marked a full revolution of the contraption. By a quarter of eleven he knew how many steps there were.

She sat down next to him without a word. Her eyes lacked the redness that comes with crying but the skin around them was puffy. A quick swipe of lipstick was all the makeup she wore.

"I hoped you'd get tired of waiting and leave," she said softly in a voice barely under control.

"What's wrong, Lynn?" he asked, placing his hand on her shoulder.

"It's Tony. He knows about us, that you spent the night at least once. I think he's having the apartment watched. Anyway, he knows."

"Was bound to happen sooner or later."

"I told you to be careful! Fix that damned muffler. Be quieter . . ." Tears began anew as she grasped for a place to lay blame.

He wanted to celebrate. They were finally out in the open. No more sneaking around. "Look, so he found out. How bad can that be?"

She clamped her gaze on him, bearing down with an intense stare. He felt suddenly trapped. Taking this lightly had been a mistake. He reached out to touch her shoulder and she drew away. "Tell me about it," he said, making no further attempt to touch her.

"Tony announced this morning when he came to get Vicky that he was going to go to court and get custody changed, that he could prove me . . . unfit." Tears started again, quiet tears of defeat.

"How can he do that? Why would he want to? He's still in the Navy — unmarried, traveling, unstable life. That's no way for Vicky to live. Are you sure he's not just blowing smoke?"

"I'm not sure of anything right now."

"Sounds like he's punishing you for having the brains and good taste to have divorced him. And besides, he'd lose his case in court. No judge in his right mind would give him Vicky."

"But why? Why now?" She held her handkerchief out, dabbing at her face.

"Hell, who knows. Maybe he's slowing down, can't catch the young skirts anymore, starting to feel lonely or domestic or just pissed off."

"But he knows about us."

"That *he* knows doesn't matter — you're divorced. Vicky doesn't know, but I'm beginning to believe that even if she did, it wouldn't matter. Think how many times she's tried to play cupid with us. 'Can Mark stay with us? Are you and Mommy getting married? Will you get me a sister?' " He smiled at the memory and added, "Tried to find her a sister but the convent was fresh out." He touched her hair. "He's just trying to bug you."

"He's doing a damned good job of it." She sniffed and wiped her nose again with the soggy handkerchief. He pulled his own from a hip pocket and handed it to her.

"Honey, why don't we get married and put an end to all this bother?"

"Oh, Mark, don't start putting that pressure on me, too. I've got to handle this myself, my own way."

"Why won't you let me help? You can get out from under Tony's thumb —"

"And under yours?" she said quickly.

He waited until his flush of anger drained away. "We

both know that's not true. This fear of what Tony may or may not do has gotten out of hand, Lynn. Look at the state you're in. Right now you're not making enough money and things are tight. Plus the cost of a lawyer if he really does sue. Okay, I understand that. But I also know that I love you and I believe in what we have together, what we can do together. Let me help." He tried drawing her closer, but felt her stiffen with resistance.

"I need time to think. I need to be alone. You understand that, don't you?"

"Sure. Besides, we've got to stop meeting like this — on the romantic escalator bench." No smile.

"It's not you, Mark. I just need some time."

"Wish this had happened before I went to sea — be two weeks ahead." He smiled and hugged her, wiping a trace of wetness from the side of her nose.

They walked to the parking lot and he watched her drive away. On cruise. How much longer would it last?

★

He finished his unnecessary housework, scrubbing again the already-clean tub and sinks, vacuuming the spotless carpet. Tom LaCroix's phone went unanswered. There was no one else to call. By two o'clock the emptiness of the weekend had become quite real.

Mark drove back to *Modoc,* deserted now but for the duty section, and settled at his desk. At least this extra time would allow him a head start preparing the Lamm case. He reviewed what evidence he had and began writing his opening argument.

The quiet of the ship closed around him. Most of the duty section, those not actually standing watches, were probably in their racks reading or playing cards. The engineers had gone "cold iron", with only an auxiliary generator on line should services from the pier be interrupted.

He had finished the first draft of the statement when a sharp knock on the metal door startled him in the silence of the small room.

"Come in," he called automatically.

The door opened slightly and Petty Officer Lamm poked his head in. "Sorry to disturb you, sir, but the OOD said you were aboard."

"Come in," he repeated, closing the case file. He waited until Lamm had taken the chair he indicated, then said, "You realize that before I can talk to you I have to give you rights all over again. Protects us both."

The petty officer leaned forward, resting his elbows on his knees. "I was hoping we could talk off the record."

Mark studied the man for a moment and reminded himself that his case could be jeopardized should he happen to violate Lamm's rights. But then, he reasoned, Lamm hasn't done anything dishonorable.

Lamm leaned back, placing his palms on his dungarees, sliding his hands forward and back as if trying to rub every trace of his fingerprints into the denim. "I've been reading up on what the procedure is all about with the discharge board and I know what you can do . . . if you want to."

"What's on your mind?"

Lamm leaned forward again. "Now that Overmiller is . . . dead . . . gone . . . whatever, I was wondering how that will affect my case. Especially since Arnold is the one responsible for him going over the side."

"Well, first, Arnold is only accused at this point."

"I heard he made a full confession."

"I really shouldn't be discussing Arnold's case at all, but I can tell you that nobody witnessed Overmiller going over. So far it's all circumstantial evidence. He still could have been pushed, but I think there's enough to establish that Overmiller fell as a result of being high on drugs supplied by Arnold." His words, as if recorded and played back on a badly echoing telephone connection, sounded formal, stiff. Mark struggled to find the correct conversational tone for an off-the-record talk. "What that means to both myself and you — or your lawyer — is that neither of us will have the opportunity to question Overmiller on the stand. I suppose that could work to your advantage."

"But, sir." Lamm squirmed in the hard chair. "I thought the accusations might be dropped since Overmiller was obviously a doper. It doesn't seem right I can't face my accuser."

It was Mark's turn to twist in his chair. "You said you studied board procedures?"

"Yes."

"Then you know that it doesn't follow trial rules. Overmiller doesn't have to be there. His statement is enough."

"A kangaroo court."

"I said it's not a court."

"What difference does it make?" Lamm asked, his face reddening.

"There *are* differences," Mark said quietly, the hollowness of the words ringing in his ears as he spoke the company line. "Your rights are —"

"Nonexistent," Lamm broke in. "Isn't that the word, Lieutenant?"

Yes, Mark thought, nonexistent. Sign the paper. Admit to being homosexual whether you are or not, save us all a lot of time. Take the discharge quietly because it's going to happen no matter what.

He drew a deep breath. Lamm had, indeed, studied the procedures. "I don't know what else I can tell you."

"You're going to be the recorder, aren't you?"

"Yes."

"What are you going to do, sir?"

"I'm going to try to prove what Overmiller said. That's my job."

"I guess I mean, how well are you going to do your job?"

"I'll do the best I can."

"But do you believe all this crap?"

"What I believe doesn't . . ." He left the sentence hanging in the still air. He knew too well what he was doing. Playing *officer,* coughing up military rhetoric — *ours is not to reason why* . . . He turned to the desk and shuffled papers about. "I have a lot of work . . ."

"Yes, sir," Lamm said with a sigh. "I understand. It's your job." He stood as Mark continued to stare at the desk before him. "I wanted to know what's in it for you."

"My career, goddamnit, my . . ." Mark jerked around to stare at the man, his eyes narrowing.

"I know how you feel. It's my career, too." Lamm drew himself up to full height, the stoop he normally affected now gone, and walked to the door. "Thanks for talking, Lieutenant," he said, almost airily. He pulled the door shut gently behind him.

"Sorry," Mark said in the empty room, barely a whisper.

✯ Chapter Thirteen ✯

MARK ROLLED on his side to escape a bothersome shaft of sunlight from his apartment window. The bedroom atmosphere had become heavy with the boxed-in heat of Sunday morning. A light film of perspiration covered his face and he kicked at the sheet over him. Dry mouth and a headache.

"Damned fool," he said aloud, acknowledging his intemperate bout with three martinis and a pair of large brandies last night after he returned from the ship. He wondered when he would hear from Lynn; she had said a couple of days.

He let the warm shower beat the back of his head and neck. But instead of massaging away his headache, the insistent, tiny drumbeat of the pulsing spray echoed through his mind. He reacted with a sudden burst of anger, slamming his palm against the tiled wall, nearly knocking himself off his feet in the slippery tub.

He faced the stream of water and let it beat on his head, then flow like a waterfall in front of his face. How could he have let Lamm draw him out, catch him off guard? He reflected on his restrained upbringing by a single mother after his father had died in combat in the early days of the Vietnam War. Mark had been five and remembered little of Gunnery Sergeant Jack Palmer, who had already been away for a year when the two Marine officers arrived at the door to announce the government's gratitude for his service.

While his mother continued to work at her beauty shop, gradually Mark had taken on greater responsibility, cleaning the house, helping with the shopping, developing independence along with self discipline and an acute appreciation for order. He had known early on that he would be a military man, perhaps in some way to avenge his father's death.

He understood that signs of his childhood were everywhere, in his obsessively spotless apartment and his attention to detail. The way each thing had to be just so in each kitchen drawer, the neat way he folded his socks and underwear — they had been among the things that had driven Cora nuts. He had come to accept his tidiness as probably a little abnormal, though it served him well in the Navy. "Never lost a cent on the cleaning deposit any time I moved," he had told Lynn. "But what do you expect from someone who can fold a fitted bedsheet and make it come out with square corners?"

He dried slowly, avoiding the mirror. He ran his hand over the stubble on his face. Needed a shave. Wouldn't. Something else to feel guilty about. Breaking his routine of morning ablutions would surely send him straight to hell, he thought sarcastically. But more threatening than hell was his outburst of his own fear in front of Lamm. Lamm — the one man who could turn it to his advantage. Lieutenant Palmer was afraid for his career — like Lamm, like everyone.

After his mother's heart attack and sudden death while he had been studying mechanical engineering in college, his cool detachment saw him through. He had loved her, though it seemed to be a love without obligation. She had been content — or at least had never complained — living alone. Without meaning to, mother and son had allowed the space between them to widen and neither had found it particularly odd. Mark hadn't spent time wondering why before, but the reasons seemed to be getting clearer now. "Warped son of a bitch . . ." The words echoed in the steamy, sterile bathroom.

★

"It isn't right, Lieutenant!" Once again Lamm stood just inside Mark's stateroom door. "I ought to be able to get my own lawyer. I don't want this one." His slender face revealed anger and uncertainty.

"I'm sure she's a competent attorney," Mark said, not knowing what else to say.

"I want the first lawyer I talked to — Lieutenant Templeman," Lamm said, crumpling the letter Mark had given him appointing Lieutenant Sandra Bellflower as his counsel.

"All right, I'll call over to the legal center and ask that he be assigned since . . . you prefer him and he already has a head start on the case. Of course, if Lieutenant Templeman isn't available . . ."

"Then I'll get a civilian lawyer," Lamm said, clenching his fists at his sides.

"All right, but I should be able to tell them why you won't accept Lieutenant Bellflower."

"I want the best chance I can get." Lamm's normally passive face tightened, his lips pressed together, puffing out the skin around his mouth. He focused his eyes on the overhead behind Mark, then released some of the tension. "I don't think it would look right to the board, like I was hiding behind my mother's skirts. Especially . . ."

"You think that being represented by a woman would cast doubts on your masculinity when the whole case is about just that, right?"

"Yes sir. And I don't want to make it any easier for you." Lamm froze, as if by his sudden silence he could keep the words from reaching Mark's ears. "Sorry, sir."

The thought of Lamm hiring a civilian lawyer doubly chilled Mark. Not only would he have to face someone who probably didn't believe in the inevitability of the outcome of the Administrative Discharge Board, but a lawyer from the city could bring media pressure to bear. In the view of most reporters we're a bunch of Neanderthals. No, he thought, better to get who Lamm wants as long as it's a JAG officer who wouldn't willingly bare the Navy's dirty laundry.

"Thank you, sir." Lamm turned to the door. "You know I'm going to fight!"

Mark waited until Lamm departed before allowing himself a smile. "Fight me, man. Fight me," he said, slamming his hand to the desk, "You won't win but you might feel better."

His mood changed in an instant. "Stupid! Oh shit, how stupid." Of course Lamm *should* have a civilian lawyer. Of course. That would take the curse off *Modoc* and me. The legal center then would have to appoint a Navy lawyer to prosecute and take it off my hands. Public Affairs officers from the Naval District would handle the press. I'd be able to watch the whole thing on television and not have to worry about Bennett scuttling my career. On top of that, the press coverage wouldn't do Bennett any good, might show him up to be the demagogue he was.

One phone call is all it would take. Mark reached for

the receiver. A small lie. Not even a lie. He could tell the legal center Lamm didn't want Lieutenant Bellflower and not mention anything about Templeman.

Still, he dropped the receiver on the cradle before the second ring and lowered his face into cupped hands. The perfect solution. Save his own career, probably Lamm's, too, with public pressure on top of the flimsy evidence. A cause that could unite the straight and gay communities. The board would be damned should they return with a recommendation for discharge. The American Civil liberties Union could stick its nose into the Navy's business screaming "unconstitutional" and be right.

Unjust accusations. Everyone could rally around that flagpole. Another chance, too, for the gays to attack the military's handling of homosexuals. They already knew how to turn the system back on itself with a phony form letter that had given every laggard and malcontent — since gays and lesbians had gotten organized — a simple, foolproof way to get out of the service.

Dear Sir,

I have committed homosexual acts while in the Navy with civilian personnel. I have committed no acts with military personnel. I am a practicing homosexual, something I recently found out about myself. When I joined the service I was not a homosexual.

I request an immediate discharge as I cannot live with the repressive, discriminatory policies of the Navy and still work to my full capacity or achieve advancement under them.

This statement is made of my own free will.

Mark remembered legal school and the Marine instructor. He had waved a copy of the well-crafted letter at the class and complained there was virtually no way to fight it. "Ignore it for a while," he said. "Make the suckers sweat. Drag your feet with the paperwork. Let them live with their admission. The story would leak out eventually through some blabbermouth yeoman handling the papers.

"Let them *suffer* a little peer pressure for three or four months. That's another three or four months of watches they can stand, paint they can chip, and decks they can swab. Besides," the Marine lawyer had commented, "the little bastards wouldn't have to *suffer* the repressive and discriminatory policies of the Navy if they had kept their mouths shut and done their cocksucking elsewhere. No stigma anymore being a fag so a little play-acting and they get out of their contract. They even get GI benefits if they've *suffered* six months. Honorable discharge if they can manage to remember their original story. The fakers are giving queers a bad name!"

The student officers had laughed uproariously.

"What about 'Don't Ask, Don't Tell?' " a student asked when the class had settled.

"You don't have to ask a thing. Those who want to get out — either the real gays or those making a false confession — are gonna *tell* plenty. The quiet ones who want to stay aboard . . . well, they are gonna piss someone off sooner or later — someone who'll drop a dime on 'em. 'Don't Ask, Don't Tell' was a gift to you from a bunch of politically correct, pantywaist, draft dodgers in Washington who have no concept of what we do or how we do it. Ladies and gentlemen, since 1994 — when Congress officially made military life gay-friendly — homosexual discharges have doubled," the major announced with a grin. "Now that's using our gifts! Of course, if they had a 'Don't Squeal' policy we'd be out of business. You can always count on *someone* who can't keep his mouth shut."

Now, Mark raised his face from his hands. Pressure from his palms had momentarily blurred his vision but he reached for the phone. He'd get Templeman "for the good of the service." Keep it in-house, quiet. He was still an officer following orders, displaying that special trust and confidence placed in him. The words, stiff as wardroom scrambled eggs, came to him. Officer Corps propaganda. Still, he had sworn to honor it and the tradition that spawned it. He dialed.

★

"Members of the board, I intend to prove the respondent did lure an innocent member of his division to his apartment for the express purpose of committing homosexual acts, violating not only the personal privacy of his victim but breaking the superior/subordinate relationship.

"It would be easy to disbelieve the allegations for a number of reasons: the mere fact that the respondent is a veteran of twelve years, the character of the complainant, to name a few. But, gentlemen, these are only mitigating factors and do nothing to deny the simple truth of the act."

Mark dropped the argument on the desk and flopped on the bunk. It kept coming out the same each time he practiced it — like a defense argument. No, he thought, this won't work, not before a board of officers raised in the tradition of the second language that set the officer corps apart from the enlisted.

The first reprimand he had received as an officer was

over his foolish wording of a memo to the executive officer on the cruiser. He had suggested a menu change in the wardroom and was informed by the tight-jawed XO that juniors may "recommend" to seniors while seniors "suggest" to juniors, and a suggestion carried the same force as an order.

The language allowed an officer to write an enlisted evaluation the sailor would love, feel good about, but another officer could detect as something less. A secret "black ball" could be hidden among other, meaningless phrases. Damnation by faint praise — a skill any officer could be proud of. For a man to be rated "above reproach" begged the question of *how far* above.

The door swung open and Dave Brown burst into the stateroom. He stood beside the bunk, hands on hips, staring down at his roommate as he would a puppy that had messed the carpet.

"Don't want to disturb your beauty rest, Lieutenant. I know how much you need it, but the skipper wants you now."

"Only reason you're bringing me such good news," Mark paused significantly and swung his feet to the deck, "is that you must have been up there with him, doing your best to get my job." He looked up at Dave and stood, shoving him with his shoulder when Dave wouldn't step aside. "Jesus, Dave, grow up! This victim shit you're pulling is getting boring." Mark set his jaw and prepared to shove again when Dave stepped back.

Time to defuse this bomb, Mark realized and gentled his voice. "I'll admit, particularly now, I'd rather be chief engineer, but I'm not doing anything to shoot you down. This job was the luck of the draw and I had bad luck, all right?"

Dave remained silent but his expression softened.

"All I ask is you let me come down and fondle an engine now and then — even an aux generator would be enough. I wouldn't want to romanticize too much, though. I've gotten used to clean uniforms. How 'bout it, roomie — can we stow this crap?"

"All right. Sorry about the static."

"Forget it. What does the old man want now?"

"Didn't say but he had *me* up there chewing my ass over the morale in my department."

★

The executive officer occupied the chair next to the commanding officer's desk. Both men faced the door as Mark knocked and entered.

Bennett didn't invite Mark to take the one vacant chair. "Frank here tells me that we have a real problem. A morale problem." He leaned back.

Mark waited for more but the silence told him it was his turn to speak. "I've heard that." Got one of my own, he thought.

Frank Madera took over from the captain. "So far this morning I've had six men put in requests to have a little chat with the captain. Four from engineering and two from deck. They all want to talk to the skipper about harassment from you, Mark."

"Are you serious, XO?"

"You bet he is," Bennett answered. "And any one of us knows when six people want to come up here and bitch, there's probably something really wrong."

"Yes, sir. There sure is." Mark felt hot blood color his neck.

Bennett leaped up. "Mister, you getting wise with me again?"

"Sorry, sir, just an observation."

"An *observation,* is it, like you're above it all, an outsider. That's the root of all this, your prima donna attitude! Too good for the rest of us mere sailors. You think you can run around this ship terrorizing the crew and ignoring the officers."

"I wasn't aware . . ."

"You expect me to believe you weren't aware of your Gestapo tactics in the Arnold case when you came in here for permission to 'fish' for evidence?"

"I didn't do anything illegal," Mark said, thinking, you gave me the permission to search the lockers; it was your decision.

"Maybe, but the morale of my crew doesn't rest on the kind of hair-splitting legalities you're so adept at. Questioning the whole crew is a little excessive, don't you think?"

"Yes, sir, I think so. But you'll remember I did it under your orders when nobody came forward — *everyone* except chiefs and officers."

"I gave no such orders!" The captain shot a look at Frank as if to convince him. He lowered his voice to a mock confidential whisper. "Mister Palmer here has been caught lying before, XO."

"Captain . . ." Mark began, edging once more toward the kind of combat he had no chance of winning.

"I haven't given you permission to speak, Lieutenant," Bennett took clear pleasure in the control he could exercise over subordinates. "Now keep your insolent mouth shut for a moment while the XO and I work this out. Right, XO?"

Frank looked uncomfortable, like a helpless witness to a highway crash. Mark felt that same humiliation he remembered as a four-year-old when his mother jerked his pants down in the produce section of the Safeway and laid her open hand hard against his buttocks. He couldn't remember what he'd done for the punishment, but he'd never forget that slap.

He watched his two superiors talk, not hearing, for blood rushed through his ears like river rapids.

". . . and I expect you at wardroom functions." Bennett's voice broke in. "Do you understand me, Mister Palmer?"

"Yes, sir," he said automatically. He'd have to ask Frank later what it was he was supposed to have understood.

☆ CHAPTER FOURTEEN ☆

MARK SAT IN HIS FIAT gazing at *Modoc.* She wasn't his ship anymore. And without more than a physical connection to a ship he was diminished, something less, like someone who could only stand on the shore and wish. The fact that he would continue to report in the morning, take her out of the harbor, and stand watches on her bridge no longer meant what it had. Bennett had chosen him to accept the blame for ship's morale. Mark remembered warning the XO that morale would suffer on the day Overmiller's letter arrived.

"What more do they want from me?" he said, bouncing his palms off the steering wheel. He reran the whole dressing down through his mind. Details surfaced that had escaped him at the time, subordinated to his anger and frustration. A martinet. The captain had called *him* a martinet, as if he had no feelings for the men. Bennett was describing himself. Am I getting like him?

He had promised himself on commissioning that he'd never forget what it was to be a bluejacket. Had he let that slip away, clinging so tightly to his new status that he failed to remember where he had come from?

"No!"

He started the engine. Frank had only nodded when he told him he'd be leaving early for the city library. Research. He was sure Frank really believed he'd be stopping at a bar to lick his wounds from the worst, most irrational chewing-out — no, officers are counseled, not chewed out — he'd ever had.

"What about *my* morale?" he asked the wind as he turned onto Harbor Drive. He worked smoothly through the gears, shifting at five thousand RPM, hitting sixty before braking for the Thirty-second Street intersection.

Both sides of Harbor were packed with characteristically bleak Navy buildings. His mind wandered to the few modern structures, the Navy Exchange, the enlisted quarters. He hadn't realized until now that they all had an emotionless look. Inside, the plumbing was exposed, painted the same color as the walls but plainly there, like the inside of a ship. Taxpayers must love it. They don't have to look at it, he thought as he watched a few sailors cross the overhead footbridge.

He moved with the green light along the heavily trafficked street toward the industrial hodgepodge under the San Diego-Coronado Bay Bridge, through a heavy veil of smell from the tuna processing plant at water's edge. The waterfront district. It was still the kind of place where Lynn snapped the door locks — even in a convertible with the top down.

Lynn. He'd call her, see how she was. After the library.

★

He stood at the checkout desk feeling slightly embarrassed, like when his mother had sent him to the drugstore at age fifteen for a box of Kotex. A big box. The library clerk completed the ritual without a word or change of emotion and handed back the five books, all containing *homosexual* or *gay* in their titles.

Sure, Mark thought, this is stupid, being embarrassed, as if I'm studying up to be gay. Yet, he made sure the titles faced the floor and the spines were hidden against his side before venturing onto the city sidewalk.

★

"Hello?" Lynn's cautious voice in his ear.

"It's me, honey. I just wanted to call and see how you were doing and maybe, you know, ah, see if we could get together, you know."

"I . . ." Silence then but for the small *tic-tic* on the phone line.

"I mean it's been three days. I could meet you at the park, you know, our regular spot. Bring Vicky. I miss her, too. All right?"

"Okay," she finally said.

"Five-thirty. I'll bring some chicken. We can have a picnic like we used to . . ." He was talking in the past tense, as if their relationship were long over.

"Okay."

The phone went dead. Had he been talking to a machine? What could have robbed Lynn of her emotion? She hadn't used more than one word at a time. What is that bastard Tony doing to her now? What is she doing to herself? He felt hairs prickle on his neck. Tony wasn't satisfied having his freedom and girlfriends; he had to make Lynn miserable, too. A real Prince Charming. If he couldn't have her, nobody else could.

He packed a bottle of cheap champagne into a wicker hamper with a can of orange soda for Vicky. He paused, thinking now about how the six-year-old girl must be reacting to this change. Lynn, sullen and upset. Himself — practically a fixture at their apartment — not around for close to three weeks.

Four-thirty. He'd have time to stop at a pet shop and pick up the fish tank set Vicky had been talking about since they had visited the Scripps Aquarium. He smiled, remembering how she had struggled with the Latin names of fish she particularly liked, insisting he repeat them until she could do the same.

Pseudotropus whatchamacallit they had dubbed one tiny neon-striped fish when they found the nameplate was missing from the front of the display. And later he and Lynn had lain in bed giggling about Vicky's fractured pronunciation. They agreed a tank would be good for her in an apartment where dogs and cats were forbidden. A birthday present, or for Christmas.

Why not now, he decided.

★

He watched them come across the grass, Vicky scuffling a cloud of dust as they reached the barren spots dotting the softball field. She spotted him and ran to where he sat at a concrete table, screaming his name. He stood and let her come to him, overalls flapping, blond hair flying. He swooped her up as she went limp, allowing his strength to carry her in a high arcing circle. He spun her twice, then sat heavily on the bench as if the exertion had drained him.

"You're turning into a real heavy lunch," he said. "Getting too big for me."

"Nope. You're getting weak." She laughed and hugged his neck.

Lynn approached, and he kept his hand on Vicky's head as he stood. "Hello, Lynn," he said, detecting something in her eyes that warned him away from the embrace that was their usual greeting.

"Hello," Her eyes focused on the box he had placed on the bench behind the table. "Vicky, go play on the swings for a while. Mark and I have to talk."

"I want to play with Mark."

"I said go play." Her voice rose with anger unmistakable to Vicky, for he felt the child tense under his hand.

"Go ahead, Vicky. We'll play later." He bent slightly and nudged her toward the swings. She went slowly, glancing back as if she had been exiled for life.

"What is that?" Lynn pointed at the box but her tone made it clear she knew precisely what the blue and yellow box contained.

"A fish tank. Aquarium," he answered matter-of-factly, and sat on the bench. The edge of the table bit into his back.

"How could you be so stupid?"

"As I recall, we agreed it would be good for Vicky since you had to give up the cat when you moved from the house."

"That was before."

"Before what? What's the harm?"

"You know she'll tell Tony. I can't make her keep quiet. And I refuse to put her in the position of having to keep my secrets."

"Secrets? What's secret about an aquarium?"

"Where she *got* the aquarium." Lynn said.

"Look, *you* give it to her. Tell her the tooth fairy brought it, I don't care what you tell her."

"You know very well she'll figure you had something to do with it. You even promised it to her. Come to the park, see you, and go home with that thing." She put her hands on her hips.

"Aw, Lynn." He reached for her hand, "Let's not be like this. I'll take it back."

She moved back half a step beyond his reach, keeping her arms stiff at her sides.

He looked in Vicky's direction. She had found another child and they sat in the sand near the swings absorbed in play. He stepped around the table and took up the box. "I'll put this in the car. There's chicken and potato salad in the hamper."

He walked across the field to his car, his thoughts as confused as a tangle of worms. How could he have suspected Lynn would see the gift as a compromise? Why *didn't* he see it? That had always been his problem — he never had been able to see beyond the surface of any relationship. Everything had to be explained to him as if his perception was like a fault map of California enmeshed with gaps and fissures.

He threw the box into the narrow backseat and pulled his jacket over it. He was losing Lynn — Vicky along with her. That he *could* see. He walked back slowly, stiffly, while the image of Lynn standing rigidly at the picnic table wavered in his sight. She was watching Vicky protectively.

"Honey," he said, reaching her, "I'm sorry about the tank. If you need more time to work things out, that's okay. I mean I won't call again."

"I know you want to help me, Mark, but you can't do it by giving Tony more ammunition to use against me. You can't do it by sneaking around at night" — her voice raised in pitch — "and you can't do it by giving Vicky presents that she'll tell him about." She turned away. "You're a liability, and I can't afford that now."

"That's what it boils down to? I'm a *liability*?"

"Can't you understand? Tony's trying to take Vicky! And you're part of the reason. I *can't* see you."

"Just like that? All over — two years down the tubes."

She didn't answer.

He felt his anger rise. "Goddamnit Lynn, are you going to let that guy run your life forever? Aren't you going to fight him, show him he can't do that?"

"Fight. That's your answer for everything, isn't it? Well, my life isn't some war game with neat rules and plastic ships you can shove around the board. The only thing that's important to me is Vicky. She's just a little girl." She sniffed. "Oh, why am I talking to you, you're just like him, barging through life like a bull, not giving a damn who you run over as long as you get what you want."

"That's not true and you know it." He couldn't think of anything else to say, how to defend himself from the woman he loved.

"All I know is what I feel."

"And that makes it right?"

"It makes it real." She brushed past him, striding toward the swings. He watched Vicky protest and try to wriggle away, but Lynn's grip steered the child toward the parked cars.

His guts felt empty, hands shaking as he watched Lynn drive away. Vicky's head barely showed above the window edge as she turned to see him. Her hands lay spread against the glass.

Mark turned to the table and began mechanically unpacking, then repacking, the basket, finally dropping the chicken and salad into the trash barrel. He had no energy left, so he sat on the bench with his elbows on the table, staring absently at a nearby couple. Their checked red and white cloth was set with china and silver candlesticks — in broad daylight. The man poured wine into long-stemmed goblets and they toasted. The woman's laugh drifted the forty feet between the tables — a laugh that assaulted Mark, mocking him.

He pulled his own champagne from the basket and ripped at the foil and the aluminum safety cap over the plastic cork. A twist and the soft pop of pressure escaping that had always signaled the beginning of something good, a shared time with Lynn, was now only an annoyance. He splashed the bubbling wine into a plastic cup and swallowed half in a gulp. It made him burp and he tasted an acid sickness. He swallowed the rest of the cupful and poured another.

He tossed back the cup, dribbling down his shirt, reigniting his anger. He snatched the champagne bottle and hurled it at the trash barrel. It trailed a bubbly stream, soaking the picnic basket and his shirtsleeve. The heavy glass clanged against the steel barrel and the couple at the other table stopped talking to stare at him.

Mark watched them turn back to their dinner, avoiding eye contact, now seeing him as disturbed, a clown.

He didn't belong here in the park with people. "Not here, not with Lynn, not in the Navy. What's left?" he asked aloud as he took the basket and walked slowly to the Fiat. He paused. "Not in the Navy? It'll get better," he said, and resumed walking in spite of the voice that nagged from a dark spot in his mind. *Liar,* was all it said.

☆ CHAPTER FIFTEEN ☆

MARK SHIFTED his AWOL bag to his left hand as he saluted and said, "I report my return aboard, sir." The OOD — a chief petty officer with a seamed face and a fringe of gray under his hatband — returned the salute. Mark hadn't met him before. His nametag read FARNUM.

"How long you been aboard, Chief?"

"Couple of weeks sir. Just before the tow out of Long Beach."

"Stuck with the midwatch already?" Mark smiled.

"Yes, sir." Farnum smiled back, humoring him.

Mark turned toward the door, then back on impulse. "Chief Farnum, would you mind talking for a moment?"

"Not at all, sir. Might keep me awake."

"Wish that were my problem."

"Sir?"

"Nothing." Mark glanced at his watch: 0245. The fog off the ocean carried a chilled wetness, a ghost rain swirling in tendrils through the glare of security lights. Silence surrounded *Modoc*'s quarterdeck. The bo'sun of the watch and the quartermaster stood a few feet away, talking softly in the heavy dampness.

"Chief, we've been having our share of trouble on *Modoc* and you've been here for part of it, but I expect you still have a fresh viewpoint. If you don't mind, I'd like to hear your candid thoughts on the subject. Just between you and me and totally confidential."

Farnum shrugged his peacoat higher around his ears, glanced at the two sailors on watch, and moved farther along the rail. Mark followed.

"Yes, sir, I don't mind talkin' about it." Turned away from the light as he was, his face had as much detail as the dark wool coat he wore. No face, only a voice in the night and the occasional glint of an eye.

Mark hoped he had read Farnum correctly as one of the old Navy chiefs who, when asked, would tell anyone, including the admiral, what was wrong with anything. Probably had a way to fix it as well. He had learned to respect the gruff old seadogs and their place between the officers and the rest of the enlisted ranks. Used to be called the Navy's backbone. The new jargon identified them as lower-level middle managers, a handle most of them resented.

"You ain't too popular, Lieutenant. Guess you know that. But neither is the dentist or the shore patrol. That's what I know about you. 'Course, I seen what went on with your man overboard investigation, and that's enough to put any manjack a little on edge. It'll pass, I suspect." He sucked a lungful of air and tilted his head a little, like a bird eyeing a worm. "You a mustang, Lieutenant?"

"NESEP." Mark responded with the acronym for the Navy Engineering and Science Education Program — one of the now-defunct opportunities for enlisted sailors to get a college degree and a commission.

"Well, either way you had some time wearing a Dixie Cup and dungarees. You know these guys ain't all stupid.

They don't all figure you're out to get them. Older guys, 'specially, been in long enough not to get all wrapped around the axle."

"What about Petty Officer Lamm?"

"That's another story. That one will give you some trouble. Lieutenant, if you can see your way clear to stop it, that'd be a right gentlemanly thing to do."

"Wish I could, Chief. Thanks."

His stateroom felt to Mark tonight exactly like what it was, a cold steel box. But the sensation was not unwelcome. By staying aboard in the stark room maybe he could become as cold and unfeeling as the sheet metal surrounding him. He had to focus his thoughts on the discharge board scheduled for two days away. He'd stay aboard until then. No reason now to go anyplace else.

He opened one of the books he'd gotten from the city library and lay on the bunk propped against the bulkhead. The fluorescent reading light cast a bluish glare on the pages — the brightest thing about the book, he decided after reading the foreword, the preface, and the opening page.

> The psychoanalytic theory attributes homosexuality to an inability to resolve issues arising during the Oedipal stage of development . . . suggestion that homosexuality is an expression of nonsexual problems, such as fear of adult responsibility.

Just what I need, he thought, stifling a yawn and sliding down the pillow to horizontal. In four minutes he was asleep.

★

"Hello, Lieutenant Templeman? This is Lieutenant Palmer calling about the Lamm case. Just wanted to be sure you got copies of everything, you know, statements, that stuff."

"Yes I have them. But there's something I don't understand . . . uh, Mark . . . it is Mark, isn't it? Well, Mark, I can't see why you're continuing with this thing. It's a big mistake."

"The CO desires it."

"Does he also *desire* to look like a fool when this thing blows up in his face? Or should I say in *your* face, since you're the recorder, the driving force behind this charade?"

"Why, Lieutenant Templeman . . . Larry, isn't it, I do believe you're trying to intimidate me."

"Unless you can resurrect your witness from Davy Jones's locker, you're going to have a tough time presenting a case to the board."

"Are you trying to appeal to my sense of fairness, Larry? This is an admin board, don't forget."

"See you Thursday, Mark," Lieutenant Templeman said with a chuckle. "Unless of course you can convince your skipper to come to his senses about this. Don't forget, Mark, this is my territory, the law. I don't attempt to run a ship's engines because I'm not a snipe, and you shouldn't attempt to beat me on my own ground."

"Larry, it's been good talking to you. Have a *nice* day." Mark dropped the receiver to the cradle.

He knew the verbal badinage was only a ploy to shake his confidence, but still, when he looked at the scant evidence and his own feelings about the case, he had little to be confident about. No wonder Lamm wanted Templeman, cocky as a recruit on home leave, to represent him. Mark's irritation grew as he considered what he now faced. He answered the phone on the second ring.

"Come up here, Mark." It was Bennett, probably ready to level another other bogus charge at him.

He had skipped breakfast and lunch while he had alternately worked on his arguments and read bits from the homosexual books. Climbing the single ladder to the 0–2 level suddenly became a task that drained his strength, taking all his effort. Weak from not eating since, since . . . lunch yesterday? No. He dismissed it. Must be tired, that's all. He sighed, gripped the handrail, and pulled with his arms up the eight rungs.

"Brief me," the captain said, rocking back in his chair.

Mark plunked down in the chair by the door. Was it his imagination or was the skipper going to listen this time? Bennett's face was relaxed; he even smiled a little. Either a changed attitude or a sneak attack. "It's coming along. Lamm has a hotshot lawyer. Lieutenant Lawrence Templeman. Said we don't have a chance and this will blow up in your face — meaning mine, too."

Mark looked up and saw the captain's large American Beauty rose directly in his line of sight to Bennett's head. A fat khaki body with a deep crimson rose head puffing smoke from a pipe. The captain swung his chair to the side to peer around the flower. "So what did you say?"

"Have a nice day."

Bennett chuckled and his chair swung back. Mark spoke directly to the rose. "It'll be a little tougher to win this case without Overmiller, but then again, maybe not."

"Why's that?" Bennett leaned forward.

"He wasn't credible. The board would never believe him. If anyone had a motive for throwing him overboard, it was me."

Bennett leaned forward and slid the heavy-based

bud vase to the opposite corner of the desk, ending the game. "Even so, I can't believe anyone would lie about homosexuality. It's so goddamned disgusting."

"Maybe so, Captain, but most males have some homosexual contact in their lives — even some animals have *gender confusion*. Think back to when you were eight or ten out in the bushes with another kid . . ."

"That's enough! I have no intention of sitting here while you spin fairy tales." The captain stood, as if ready to upbraid Mark again, then thought better of it and sank back behind the desk.

Mark slouched in the chair, something he would never have considered a week before. "As you know, Skipper, I've made a request to SURFPAC to assign an officer to act as the third member of the admin discharge board. He'll be senior member — has to be a lieutenant commander or above, and we can't use you or the XO. He's a commander. Name is Sam Penny. He'll be here tomorrow at 1400 to meet the other board members and get a briefing from me on procedure. You want to see him? You know, to thank him for his time?"

Puzzlement crossed Bennett's face, obviously confused by Mark's change of subject and lack of response to the captain's implicit threat. "Yes, I suppose so. Yes, yes, that would be a good idea."

"All right, sir, I'll bring him up here soon as he arrives." He straightened in the chair. "Anything else, Captain?"

"Ah, who did you assign as the other two members? I'll want to talk to them."

"Lieutenant Tapia and Lieutenant junior grade Kastner." Mark rose, walked to the captain's desk and placed his knuckles on the blotter, leaning forward to within a foot of the captain's face. He lowered his voice. "I wouldn't want to see them together. Might look like you're trying to influence the outcome of the board. I'll ask them to come up separately." He didn't wait for an answer before he slipped out the door.

His heart thumped. He had handled Bennett, finally, without being overtly threatened by him, by taking the offensive. But there was no joy in it, rather a feeling of loss. It meant nothing that the senior member was from somewhere else. Will Tapia and Bert Kastner could outvote him. After all, they had to live with *Modoc* and Bennett. Maybe the old man will try to steer Penny, too. If he does and Penny has any balls he'll report it to SURFPAC — for the good it'll do.

Don't count on it, a voice inside his head reminded him. He climbed down the ladder and into his stateroom. It had begun to smell the way it did at sea, with two men and their laundry sharing the tiny box.

He dialed operations. "Will? Sometime this afternoon the old man would like to see you."

Mark imagined the man on the other phone, the oversized jock, college football player, arms like smoked hams.

"I still haven't thanked you for sticking me with this admin board," Will said. "All right, I'll go. Day's been going too well anyway. You got any more good news? Earthquake, airplane crash, hurricane?"

"Some woman's waiting for you on the quarterdeck with a baby she swears is yours."

"Funny," came Will's reply.

Mark made another call to Bert Kastner in supply. The conversation lacked the spirit of the one with Will. Bert was humorless, straightforward, plain as his rimless glasses. But a good pork chop. Knew exactly what supplies were on board and where they were and when to order more. He drove his men crazy with his ability to find what they couldn't in the labyrinth of storage spaces. Bert never made excuses; he produced the requested item. Nobody asked how or wanted to know.

☆ Chapter Sixteen ☆

"This board is convened for the purpose of considering the pertinent facts relating to the case of Marion Arthur Lamm, a thirty-four-year-old Machinist's Mate First Class, for alleged homosexual harassment of a subordinate. The following rights apply: to appear before the board, to challenge any voting member for cause, to submit an oral or written statement . . ."

Mark followed his own copy of the format as Commander Sam Penny read the text. Everyone else in the borrowed classroom at Fleet Training Center followed as well, except Chief Brown, who stood by the door acting as bailiff.

The tables were arranged in a *U* with Mark at one leg facing Lamm and Lieutenant Templeman at the other. The board members were seated across the connecting end. A single chair in the slot between them would hold witnesses.

Just like the diagram, Mark thought.

"The proceedings are administrative in nature and the board is not bound by the rules of evidence.

"And the Privacy Act of 1974 also applies. There is no requirement to provide information to the board;

however, failure to do so may deprive the board and other authorities of information which would be considered in your behalf in making recommendations and determinations in your case."

Privacy Act. Entitled to your privacy, but saying nothing is construed as having something to hide. Insidious little item, Mark thought.

Across the gap between the tables he watched Lamm sit quietly, fingers busy with each other, rubbing at rough spots, tugging cuticles. Red eyes and a darkness around them suggested he hadn't slept. The petty officer clearly struggled to project a confident demeanor but looked drawn, his normal tan appearing waxy, as if he would like to rest his head on the table and sleep through the ordeal ahead.

Beside Lamm, Lieutenant Templeman, counsel for the respondent, sat sideways in his chair, one arm slung over the back and the other sprawled across the table. He clutched a pencil lightly at one end, let his fingers slide down to the yellow pad beneath, turned the pencil over and began again. The motion hypnotized Mark, drawing his attention to the regular rhythm of taps each time the pencil touched the pad.

Though Templeman's format book was open and he faced the board, his eyes were focused elsewhere, not quite concealing his disdain for the proceedings. His almost-blond hair had been combed and carefully held in place. Hair spray? A little long for regulations, but the lawyers seemed to belong to their own Navy. Like the medical officers. Mark caught himself spending his thoughts on these trivial irritations and searched the page for the spot Penny had reached.

". . . no formal ruling on objections will be made by the senior member, but all objections and reasons for them will be made part of the official record for consideration by the review authorities."

Commander Samuel Penny looked the part of senior member. His haircut would pass a Marine inspection. In silhouette against the white projection screen behind him, his head seemed to have solid corners at the top — as though his crown had been sliced off cleanly to keep him under some height restriction. On his tailored khaki shirt he wore five rows of ribbons — fruit salad — campaign and personal decorations. Above the ribbons a gold Surface Warfare pin that bespoke his qualifications for naval combat shone dully under the fluorescent lights.

He spoke slowly, clearly, with a hint of accent. Alabama, Mark guessed. Penny projected the image of a man who could keep a ship off the rocks.

"You have the right to challenge any voting member of the board." He lowered the script and looked at Mark. "Does the recorder have any questions for the members?"

"No, sir," Mark said, straightening his chair.

"Respondent?" Penny asked.

Templeman stood, checked the tuck of his khaki shirt.

"Yes, sir. And we wish to begin with the junior member, Lieutenant Kastner."

Bert sat up but without apparent concern. He drew his shoulders back as if facing a firing squad armed with water guns, and grinned.

"You are the supply officer on USS *Modoc*?"

Bert dipped his chin slightly.

Templeman let an exasperated look cross his face, glanced at Casso operating a tape recorder on a small table in the corner, then back to the senior member. "Let the record show Lieutenant Kastner answered in the affirmative." He paused, glanced again around the room, locking eyes with each participant, save Lamm, for an instant. "Commander Penny, I respectfully request you instruct all witnesses and officers of the board to reply audibly to questions so nods and shakes don't have to be interpreted for the record."

"Very well, Lieutenant Templeman, all present are so instructed and I will instruct witnesses as they are called. Please continue with *voir dire.*"

From Templeman's expression it was clear he hadn't expected Penny to answer with such authority, even using legal terms.

"Thank you, sir. Lieutenant Kastner, is there any reason you can think of that might prejudice you in this case or render you unable to make a judgment based on facts alone?"

"No," Bert said, louder than necessary, leaning toward the microphone placed before the senior member.

"Thank you." He turned to Will. "Lieutenant Tapia, I would like your answer to the same question."

"No."

"Do you know the respondent?"

"I've seen him, know who he is, but nothing intimate."

Silence filled the room like smoke in a pool hall. Will looked puzzled after a few seconds, seeing every eye upon him. His eyes darted back and forth as if he were reading a transcript of what he had just said. "By intimate I mean I've never talked to him." The color rose in his cheeks as he continued past the point he should have stopped. "You know, I don't mean like intimate with a woman, or anything like that."

"I think we know what you mean, Lieutenant," Penny cut in.

Templeman was back in his seat, whispering to

Lamm, then listening for a whispered answer. "No challenges," Templeman said.

★

"Gentlemen of the board," Mark began his opening statement, "Petty Officer Lamm lured a young sailor from his division to his apartment in National City, plied him with alcohol and pornographic films, then made a homosexual advance. By breaching the traditional superior/subordinate relationship, such an act is a direct assault on the trust and credibility of all leaders.

"We are not here to avenge the sexual honor of a single sailor. That would be foolish, considering the victim of the assault was tragically lost at sea. No, gentlemen, we are here to protect ourselves and every other man and woman who wears the badge of authority. One man, Petty Officer Marion Arthur Lamm, broke the trust we have all worked for. We cannot dismiss it as an isolated case.

"We have here an act that sets in motion a cancerous web of fears and suspicions among all crewmen. An example. Just one small indication of the far-reaching effects of Petty Officer Lamm's act. The enlisted heads aboard *Modoc* have begun sporting a new theme in graffiti. 'Take the steak and run,' says one, alluding to the welcome-aboard dinner Petty Officer Lamm used to lure Fireman Overmiller to his apartment. Will other similar gestures of camaraderie by senior people now be met with suspicion and skepticism?

" 'Beware the wolf in Lamm's clothing,' reads another bit of graffiti. We all know, as leaders, that when a subject such as this makes its way to toilet stalls, it is because it has caused a deep stirring of emotions among the crew. They are angry or afraid. They must be reassured that they will be protected from unwanted advances from seniors, that in the deepest sense of the word, truly, the Navy takes care of its own."

Mark laid the typewritten pages aside and glanced around the room. The board sat silent, still. Lamm picked at his fingernails and Templeman idly scratched at his yellow tablet with a felt tip pen.

He wondered if he had gone too far, prejudiced his case by coming on too strong at the outset. He didn't know, couldn't know until it was all over. And when it was over, he'd know a lot more about his own life. In two years he might be wearing a gold oak leaf on his collar or be searching for a new job. He looked again at the faces, the uniforms. The faces changed through the years but the uniform stayed constant. It comforted him to see other men sharing the same tailoring. A brotherhood of security that was always there. He couldn't allow himself to lose that.

"Gentlemen of the board." Templeman was on his feet. "I sincerely hope that what we just heard from Lieutenant Palmer is not representative of what he will be presenting during the remainder of this proceeding. I would assume, if he plans to pursue this course of argument and insists on carrying through with his frivolous allegations against Petty Officer Lamm, that he will at least produce some facts, some evidence that you can see and touch. Maybe he plans a tour for us all through the enlisted heads on *Modoc* where we can marvel at the poetry put there by who-knows-what phantom Magic Marker. Maybe the lieutenant's own.

"Are these his facts? He would have you cringe in terror that Petty Officer Lamm inhabits the same earth with you. Single-handedly, according to Lieutenant Palmer, Petty Officer Lamm has destroyed your ability to lead and the willingness of your subordinates to follow. Quite a task for a solitary petty officer. We have here a simple case. One man alleges that another made a homosexual advance. That's all.

"First you should consider the character of the two men. Petty Officer Lamm is college-educated, like yourselves, a veteran of twelve years of service. Medals, citations. Not *one* black mark!

"Now let's examine the character of Fireman Overmiller, barely a high school graduate with less than a year's service. A goof-off by any measure. Oh yes, an alcohol abuser and a drug user, too.

"Now let's talk about rights. My client was subjected to a search of his off-base private residence and belongings, and somehow details of the charges were leaked to the crew. Now *there* is the source of Lieutenant Palmer's graffiti. His own office."

Mark glanced at Casso, who was glaring angrily at Templeman. Can't blame him for being pissed, Mark thought, we both handled it as confidentially as we could. If anybody leaked it, it must have been Overmiller.

"The whole proceeding seems to be more along the lines of persecution than prosecution. And the question I have is why? What accounts for Lieutenant Palmer's zeal? Does he get a raise in pay? A promotion?"

Mark stiffened in his chair. Lamm looked up, surprised. His eyes said he hadn't discussed their private, off-the-record meeting, that Templeman must have hit upon the subject by chance. "Lieutenant Templeman," Penny cut in, angry, "you will confine yourself to the case. I won't tolerate personal attacks."

"Yes, sir," Templeman said without hesitation or emotion, as if assenting to sugar and cream in his coffee. "Because of the circumstances that leave us unable to question the one and only witness to the alleged incident in this case, I respectfully request the board declare my client innocent due to lack of evidence."

Again the room fell silent.

"Is that all, Lieutenant Templeman?" Penny spoke softly.

"Yes, sir." He remained standing.

"Then please have a seat and listen closely. You have a copy of the format and instructions; I'm surprised you didn't bother to read them. This is not a trial. The board does not deal in innocence or guilt since there is no way to punish a guilty party. We merely listen to testimony and make a recommendation as to our beliefs in the case and what we think should be done as a result. We recommend discharge or retention. Lieutenant Templeman, Lieutenant Palmer, you will both do well to remember this is an administrative, not a judicial, board." He glanced at his watch while allowing his warning to sink in.

Mark felt he was unfairly included in Templeman's dressing-down but recognized it was the only way Penny could reprimand an officer without committing the unforgivable sin of singling him out before a roomful of others.

"Let the record show the board recessed for lunch at 1145. We will continue at 1300."

Mark watched the rest leave the room. He wasn't hungry, hadn't been for several days. Ought to eat something.

"Sir?" It was Casso.

"What is it?"

"Fireman Rambo is in the passageway." He moved closer and lowered his voice. "Says he wants to testify, that Lamm made an advance to him."

"Rambo?" Mark couldn't put a face to the name, although he remembered it from the Overmiller investigation "Why didn't he say something on the ship? Why wait until now?"

"Don't know, but he's here. You want to see him?"

"Do I have a choice?" He looked at Casso. They both knew the answer. "Tell him to sit tight. I'll be out in a minute."

Mark leaned back in the chair, interlaced his fingers behind his neck and stretched, moving from side to side, bringing slight relief from the dull pain that had settled in the middle of his back. Here was a godsend — if ill timed — a live witness with his own story to corroborate Overmiller's. Then why did it feel so goddamned awful? Why did he feel deflated?

Shouting and thumping from the passageway shook him from his thoughts. He raced out. Casso and Templeman were pulling Lamm away from Rambo, dragging him upright from the floor. The fireman had skittered backward like a crab and sat huddled against a bench, his hand over his nose. Spots of blood stained his blue chambray shirt.

☆ Chapter Seventeen ☆

Purcell Rambo, Fireman Apprentice, A and E Division. Mark searched his mind for more, some recollection from the mass questioning on the ship, but he remembered little as he stood in the passageway, waiting for the teenager in the head to finish cleaning himself up.

The door opened a few inches and Rambo peered out as if expecting another attack, a shock of red hair preceding a broadly freckled nose.

"Let's get on with it," Mark said, irritation crackling in his voice. "There isn't much time."

As they walked to the Navy Exchange cafeteria on the harbor tug quay, the sailor spoke softly. "All I wanted to do was what was right, suh. I din' know Lamm was gonna beat my head in."

"Why do you suppose he did that?" Mark concentrated on listening to what the young sailor said rather than how he said it. He had never liked the slow, deep-south accent and he had to stifle the urge to slap it out of Rambo. Faster! Faster!

"I guess he don' cotton to the prospect of me tellin' y'all 'bout what he tried doin' to me."

"You mean a homosexual advance?"

"Yassuh."

"Before I put you on the stand to testify, you better convince me you're telling the truth."

Mark tried to ignore the stale grease smell of the cafeteria and the line of men and women waiting for hamburgers and fried tacos. He grabbed a pre-made tuna sandwich and a carton of milk. Rambo did the same, following him to a table in the corner.

Mark told himself that his distaste for sharing a table with the sailor had nothing to do with officer superiority. If he were a fireman himself in A and E Division, he wouldn't have chosen to sit with Rambo. The man's uniform revealed a slovenliness that even a deck hand needn't display. A shadow of beard missed by the razor darkened a patch under his jawline and he reeked of cigarettes. But Mark needed to eat and talk at the same time.

He bit deeply into the sandwich and felt immediately nauseated. Fighting down the wave of revulsion, he studied Rambo's face. A dollop of mayonnaise clung to each corner of the sailor's mouth and an arc of milk stained his face like a white moon rising over his lip.

"Jesus, Rambo, wipe your mouth."

Rambo's eyes widened, but he reached for a napkin from the container on the table and rubbed it across his mouth, leaving his sallow skin white from the pressure.

Mark looked down at his own sandwich damp with age, and tossed it into a large plastic garbage can a few feet away. Rising, wishing to escape from his aborted lunch, he moved to the door, while Rambo tossed *his* lunch remains into the can. A few drops of milk splashed back on his shirtsleeves and face.

"Feelin' okay, Loooten-ant?"

"Sure, yeah. Okay, what do you have to say? In less than an hour we're back in session."

"Yassuh," Rambo said, warming, "Y'all gonna like this."

★

Templeman shot to his feet, "I object most strenuously to Lieutenant Palmer's television-lawyer tactics — calling in a surprise witness at the last moment. I haven't had an opportunity to see any statements or to review the witness's service record. How can I properly defend my client? I want a chance to prepare and I request a continuance."

"Lieutenant Palmer?" Penny turned toward Mark.

"I submit that since this witness came to my attention little more than an hour ago, he is nearly as much a surprise to me as to counsel. I have called him hoping for your indulgence so this case can be completed as rapidly as possible. The witness hasn't made a formal statement of any kind to me but has offered what I feel to be pertinent information."

Penny glanced at Will and Bert before addressing Mark and Templeman. "As you both know, I cannot make rulings to sustain or overrule objections. And while I hesitate in this matter, I am bound to note counsel's objection for the record, and continue. Call your witness, Lieutenant Palmer."

Chief Brown swung the door open. "Rambo."

Rambo entered, took the oath, and sat down in the witness chair.

"Fireman Rambo," Mark started, "please tell the board what you know that may shed light on the case at hand."

" 'Bout a year ago when I checked in, I got assigned to Lamm's division. He tol' me that he usually takes the new guys to his place and gives 'em a dinner and some drinks and gets to know 'em and he asked me to come over. He made some fried chicken and gravy and we had some beers. We talked 'bout where I come from, down near Mobile. He said he was stationed in Pensacola for a while and knowed the area. We had some more beers and got pretty drunk. We wasn't worried 'bout gettin' back in the mornin' 'cause it was Friday night and neither of us had the duty the next day. Anyways, I started feelin' pretty woozy and he tol' me to lay down on the bed. So I went inta the bedroom and flopped down on top of the covers."

Mark watched Lamm during Rambo's testimony. His hands were now still, spread before him on the table, jaw tight, clearly on the edge of losing control.

"Later I woke up and his arm was over my shoulder. He was on the bed with me, sorta' behind me, ya' know. I pushed him off and tried to go back to sleep. I figgered he was asleep too and didn't know what he was doin'. But he come up close again pushin' into me, sorta' and runnin' his fingers down my side real slow like. I knowed he weren't asleep then. So I tol' him I din't want nothing like that. He kep' at it, talkin', you know, like I was a girl. Kep' pushin'. Finally I got pissed an' got outta' there. Got a taxi back to the ship."

Mark listened to Rambo as he spoke, the trace of nervousness in his voice gradually decreasing. He hadn't believed Lamm to be guilty until now, but his doubts began to melt away as Rambo continued his testimony.

"Do you remember the date this happened?" he asked the sailor.

"Yassuh, March the sixth."

"You seem pretty certain about that, a day over a year ago."

"I remember exactly 'cause it was Gramma Rambo's birthday that Sunday and I called her. I allus call her then." He smiled up at Mark as if he had a reward coming.

"What happened in the passageway outside this room earlier today?"

"Objection. What happened today has no bearing on this case," Templeman interrupted.

"Noted for the record," Penny said, "Continue with your direct examination, Lieutenant Palmer. Witness, answer the question."

"Well, when Lamm come out of here this mornin', he saw me and started swingin'." He held out the material of his chambray shirt. "Still got some blood here."

"Why do you suppose Lamm hit you?"

"Objection. Calls for speculation by the witness."

"Noted, continue."

"I guess he figured I was gonna tell you 'bout what happened at his place."

"Why did you wait until today to come forward? You knew about this board and the investigation earlier, didn't you?"

"Well, I was scared. What happened to Overmiller and all, and I was afraid Lamm would throw me overboard . . ."

"Objection!" Templeman was on his feet. "I object to this whole line of questioning. Petty Officer Lamm was cleared of responsibility in Overmiller's death. This is nothing but innuendo."

"Noted for the record, Lieutenant Templeman."

"Fireman Rambo, did you know Lamm's been cleared in Overmiller's death?" asked Mark.

"Nosuh."

"So you feared for your own safety?"

"Yassuh."

"I have nothing further at this time, sir." Mark dropped into the chair, his heart pumping. Progress. The objections were valid, he conceded, but they would go before a review board in Washington. They had the final say. They'd sort it out.

"Counsel for the respondent, do you wish to cross-examine the witness?"

"Yes, sir, I do." Color flushed Templeman's face as he stood. He tugged his shirt front straight and tucked it tightly under his belt. "Fireman Rambo, it took a lot of courage for you to come forward as you did today, in fear for your life, as you say, to testify. Are you aware that whatever the outcome of this board, Petty Officer Lamm will return to the ship for, oh, at a minimum, two or three months?" Rambo shot a worried look at Mark, pleading with his eyes.

"Objection. Counsel is threatening the witness."

"Yes, it's true," Templeman said. "Even in the unlikely case this board finds Petty Officer Lamm to be a homosexual he will have to be retained aboard *Modoc* until the Naval Military Personnel Command has ruled on the recommendation." He lifted a sheaf of papers from the table and pointed them at Rambo. "That's what it says here in the SECNAV Instruction. Just thought you'd like to know."

"What are you getting at, Lieutenant?" said Penny. "I won't allow you to continue to intimidate the witness."

"Sir, I am trying to establish the witness's motivation

for testifying. Fireman Rambo is obviously very courageous, not fearful as he would have us believe. It seems it would have been much safer for him to remain silent.

"Why *did* you come forward?" Templeman asked the sailor.

"It was the right thing to do."

"That's very admirable, Fireman Rambo, as is your recall of the date you spent the night — rather part of the night — at Petty Officer Lamm's apartment. What was it again?"

"March the sixth."

"Last year? You're sure about that? No question?"

"Yassuh," Rambo said quietly.

"Petty Officer Lamm tells me he was on leave during the entire month of March, and that he spent that particular evening visiting his parents in Beloit, Wisconsin."

Rambo lurched in the chair, glanced at Mark, then at the board.

"If the board wishes to verify what I've just said, the endorsed leave orders are on the left side of the respondent's service record."

Penny flipped open the record and thumbed the pages. Mark cursed himself for his stupidity. He should have known it was all too easy, too convenient. Nothing else had come easily in this case, why should this?

He looked up. Templeman stared at him, grinning, pinning him to the wall with his eyes. All his indignation had been so much acting. He had known from the beginning that Rambo had lied. Templeman was his own version of the television lawyer.

Lamm put his hands together on the table and cast his gaze at a point over Mark's shoulder, his face relaxed, confident, with a trace of smile.

"Very well, the board notes leave papers as indicated.

Fireman Rambo," Penny continued, "your conduct before the board has been noted with extreme displeasure. I will recommend to your commanding officer you be charged with making false official statements. I further want to express my total revulsion at your actions for whatever purpose you hoped to accomplish. You are advised that you are not to speak of this case to anyone outside this hearing room. The board will recess for ten minutes."

They filed into the passageway. Mark caught up with Rambo, steering him into the head.

"Wha'cha doin', Loootenant?" Rambo struggled to free himself from Mark's grasp as he found himself shoved roughly against a line of washbasins.

"You listen to me, you little bastard. You lied to me and you lied to the board. I'm going to personally write the report chit on you and I'll, by God, make it stick. Next board you sit before will be a court-martial. Now I want the truth and I want it fast. Talk." He stepped back a pace.

Rambo rubbed his arm where Mark had squeezed it and tried to brush the new wrinkles out of the blue chambray. "You can't push me 'round, *suh,* there's regulations."

"Who's going to believe I did a goddamned thing to you, dirtbag? You just became a certified liar — under oath. Now I want the truth."

Rambo glanced around the room, at the white stalls, the door behind Mark. "Lamm was buggin' ev'ryone. Allus pokin' 'round, lookin' for drugs, gettin' in ev'ryone's way."

"So some of you boys cooked up this homosexual story, right? Overmiller was lying, too."

"Nosuh. That really happened. Made him real shaky."

"How do I know you're not lying about that, too?"

"He tol' me 'bout it."

Mark laughed. "And that makes it the truth? Are you still trying to jerk me off or are you really that stupid, Rambo? I've got no reason to believe anything you say, and so far you haven't said anything I didn't already know. I got a good mind to set Lamm loose and point him at you."

"Nosuh, you can't do that, you jus' can't do that. He'll kill me sure."

"That's why he slugged you today — because he knew you were here to tell filthy lies, to put him away. Anything it took! Isn't that right, Rambo?"

Rambo's silence finally spoke the truth.

The door bumped open and Templeman sauntered in. "Sorry to interrupt, but we're expected back in a few minutes and nature calls." He walked to the urinal and unzipped.

Mark watched him for a moment, then turned back to Rambo. "You best do some fast thinking, Rambo. I want to see you in my stateroom Monday morning at 1000 sharp. You got that?"

"Yassuh."

"Now get back to the ship and report to your department. I know the time and I'll check, so don't get lost on the way."

Rambo scurried out as Templeman stepped up to the basins. "I see you and your star witness had a few crossed wires, Markie."

"Shove it."

The lawyer rinsed his hands and yanked a towel from the white dispenser. "Really stepped on your dick this time, Markie. Figuratively speaking, of course." He rolled the towel into a ball and tossed it fifteen feet into the trash-can without touching the sides. "Two points," he said, congratulating himself as he pushed through the swinging door.

Will Tapia walked in, the impassive face he wore sitting at Penny's side now replaced with a grin. "Your new office? I like it, Mark, really like it. Spacious, airy, all in chrome and white." The big officer held one wrist limply at his side and minced across the floor.

"Jesus Christ, Will, give me a break."

"Oh, you're getting a break," Will said, now serious. "Considering the floor show you just put on. You really didn't need that. Know what I mean?" He twisted his face into an exaggerated wink.

"No." Mark bristled. "What *do* you mean?"

"Back off. Hey, take it easy."

"Will, listen to me. What if Lamm *is* innocent — this whole thing *is* a setup, a conspiracy by some of the dopers on the ship to get him out of the way? Rambo was lying. Overmiller probably was, too. We know he was a drug user and Lamm was on his trail."

"Look, buddy, don't go getting noble all of a sudden with a lot of crap about right or wrong. Think of the future." He locked eyes with his friend. "Fuck this up and none of us have one. *Capice?*"

"Doesn't it even piss you off?"

"Roll with it, cowboy." He placed a large hand on Mark's shoulder. "Come on, let's get this over with."

✯ Chapter Eighteen ✯

"PLEASE STATE YOUR NAME, rating, and command for the board."

"Machinist's Mate Chief, Hector R. Vega, USS *Modoc.*"

Mark swore him in, thinking it was probably another mistake to call Vega to testify. But who else do I have? Dead witnesses are a hell of a handicap. And after Chief Vega testified that the search of Lamm's apartment had been futile, that the two civilian men had refused to talk, and that Lamm ranked as a sterling member of the ship's crew, Mark knew he had predicted correctly. If he kept questioning Vega, he'd be making Templeman's case for him. The only other chance might be during cross-examination of Templeman's witness, *Mister* Ronald Kintner. Who in hell was he? A civilian. No address, no phone number given. No chance to learn anything about him. Not like a sailor whose record you could pull and find out almost every detail about him, down to whether he'd been circumcised — in the box marked IDENTIFYING SCARS, page one. No, Kintner would be as big a surprise as Rambo.

"Thank you, Chief." Mark turned to Penny. "That's all I have for now, sir."

"Lieutenant Templeman, do you have questions for the witness?"

"Indeed I do, sir, indeed I do. Permission to approach the witness?"

Templeman walked slowly around the table into the narrow slot by the witness chair and sat on the table, one foot on the floor and his knee nearly touching Vega's elbow. "Chief Vega, I'll try to be as brief as possible."

Vega looked at the lawyer and shifted in the chair. Mark could see only the side of his face. What kind of trick was Templeman up to now, playing cozy with the witness?

"Chief Vega, who, in your opinion, is the best man you have working for you in your department?"

"Lamm."

"Thanks. Who takes over your job when you're gone?"

"Lamm."

"Thanks. Who has made it tough on marijuana smokers on the ship?"

"Lamm has, that's for sure."

"Thank you. And who did you persuade the engineering officer to recommend for the Limited Duty Officer program?"

"Lamm."

"Do you believe Lamm is a homosexual?"

"No. That's crazy."

"Thank you, Chief Vega. No further questions." Templeman returned to his seat, grinned at Mark, raised his eyebrows.

"Lieutenant Palmer, do you have redirect questions?" Penny's voice contained the slightest hint of irritation. It was growing late and obviously the board wouldn't be able to hear arguments today.

"Nothing further for this witness, sir. I have no other witnesses to call."

Everyone watched Vega move slowly to the door, stop, stare at Lamm, and raise his hand slightly. A tiny movement of his fingers, a little wave. Lamm nodded in return. Then Vega was gone.

Chief Brown leaned into the passageway. "Mister Ronald Kintner." He stepped back, and a well-built man wearing a security guard uniform walked into the room, paused, waiting for instructions.

Blue Skivvies! The man at the apartment during the search. The uniforms, Agent Berquist's supposed ace in the hole.

Mark's mind raced back to his investigation. He had assumed that because the pair of civilians in Lamm's apartment hadn't talked during the search that they never would. He hadn't followed up and gotten the whole story. In the turmoil of Overmiller's loss, Mark hadn't even asked Lamm about the men. And this is the payoff. *Surprise, idiot!*

Templeman stood quickly. His chair tipped backward and *clonked* to the floor. He ignored it and leaned forward, placing his extended fingers on the table like a pair of spiders. "What is your relationship to Petty Officer Lamm?"

"We're roommates, share an apartment together."

"We heard in earlier testimony that on the day the apartment was searched there were two men there. Were you one of the men?"

"Yes."

"And the other?"

"My brother. He got in from San Francisco the night before and needed a place to stay until he could get a job."

"So he stayed with you and Petty Officer Lamm. What were the sleeping arrangements in the apartment?"

"Well, there's a double bed and a couch."

"Do you share the double bed with Petty Officer Lamm?"

"Oh no. That was part of the deal when I moved in. See, I mostly work nights so I sleep during the day when he's at work. When we're both there together, I get the couch. He says he can't sleep with someone else in the bed. It's his apartment and I agreed to take the couch. It ain't so bad."

"What is your usual occupation, Mister Kintner?"

"Security guard."

"As we can see by your uniform. What other jobs have you held that require a uniform?"

"Gas station attendant. I worked at McDonald's for a while, still do sometimes when they're short."

"Where do you keep your uniforms?"

"In a closet at the apartment."

"Forgive me, Mister Kintner, but I have to ask a personal question. Are you a homosexual?"

"No," he said firmly.

"To your knowledge, is Petty Officer Lamm a homosexual?"

"No."

"Thank you. No further questions."

Kintner stood.

"Please, Mister Kintner, remain seated." Penny stopped him. "The recorder, Lieutenant Palmer, may have some questions."

"You mean I ain't done?" He looked across at Templeman, then to Lamm. "You didn't say nothing about answering any other questions."

"Mister Kintner," Penny interjected, "please be seated and I will explain the procedure here."

Kintner slowly sat, skepticism painted across his face.

"Whenever a witness gives testimony for or against the accused, both sides have the option of asking questions. I'm sure you have seen it on television."

"But he said this wasn't a court," Kintner protested, pointing at Templeman.

Penny smiled and stared directly at Templeman. "I'm glad of that, and he's right, it's not a court, but we do share some similarities. I'm sure Lieutenant Templeman didn't mean to mislead you. This board has no power to hold you here since you're a civilian. However, if Lieutenant Palmer doesn't have the opportunity to question you, I'll have to strike everything you've said from the record and disregard your testimony, as if you were never here."

Mark allowed himself to feel hopeful for a moment. What did Kintner have to be afraid of? He searched his memory for the key in the string of questions. His mind kept darting to the scene in the head with Templeman. He fought the urge to call across the room. "Really stepped on your dick this time, Larry."

"Mister Kintner, are you staying?"

"Excuse me, sir." Templeman interjected. "May I have a word privately with the witness? I think I can straighten out this little misunderstanding."

"Very well, Lieutenant, but make it quick. It's nearing 1600 and I would like to finish with this witness today."

"Yes, sir." Templeman walked with Kintner to the door and into the passageway.

Mark tried to recall the questions Templeman had asked Kintner: shared apartment, brother from San Francisco, sleeping arrangements, usual occupation, uniforms, you a homo? Lamm homo? The words stared back at him from the yellow pad. He let his eyes cross, blur, the letters he had written became fuzzy then watery, sloshing together in a yellow bathtub. He let them spill into his mind as he searched for the significant one that would stick crosswise in the drain as the rest flowed out.

"Lieutenant Palmer! I asked whether you wished to cross-examine the witness."

Kintner was back in the witness chair, staring at him. Templeman scribbled away, seemingly uninterested.

"Yes, sir. Permission to approach the witness, sir?"

It had worked for Templeman with Vega. Why not give it a try, Mark thought. He walked around the table and stood at Kintner's side. The man had to look up at him.

"Thanks for electing to stay for my questions."

"Ah, it's okay."

"Are you on your way to work this evening?"

"Ah, no."

"Oh, I see, you must have just gotten off work before coming here and didn't have time to change from your uniform. Is that right?"

"Uh, no."

"Let's see, you're not going to work and you haven't just gotten off work. That must mean that you normally wear your uniform during the day instead of civilian clothing. That right?"

Kintner lowered his head. "No."

"Well, then why are you wearing that uniform today?"

"Mr. Templeman told me to."

"When was the last time you worked as a security guard?"

"Christmas."

"Over four months ago. Where are you working now?"

"I'm not."

"Not even at McDonald's when they're short?"

"They haven't *been* short."

"Are you collecting unemployment benefits?"

"No. They say I don't qualify, that I haven't worked enough." Kintner was angry now. "What about when you can't get work? What about that? They don't ever think about that."

"I object. I see no point to this line of questioning," Templeman shouted.

"I do, Lieutenant," Penny snapped, "Your objection is noted for the record."

"Well, I get little jobs here and there, you know, sticking flyers under windshield wipers outside shopping centers, delivering papers, that kind of stuff."

"Doesn't pay much, does it?"

"No, don't even make my share of the rent."

"So you are more or less dependent on Petty Officer Lamm for your living?"

Kintner lowered his eyes. "Yeah, and he's been real good about it, too. I owe him a lot."

"Yes, I'd say you do. Your loyalty is evident. How did you meet Petty Officer Lamm?"

"I seen him in a bar a couple of times. One night we got to talking. I had just lost my pad. Well, it wasn't mine, really. I had a girlfriend but she kicked me out. Anyways, he wanted to cut his expenses and said I could live with him if I followed his rules and paid half the rent and food."

"So you moved in with him."

"Yes."

"When was that?"

"Last August."

"You were working steady then?"

"Yes."

"Were you there when he brought home new men from the ship for his welcome aboard dinners?"

"No. I had to stay away. That was his rule."

"That certainly seems rude of him. Did he explain why he wanted you out?"

Kintner waved his hand, dismissing Mark's observation. "Ah, it wasn't no big thing. Anyways, he said it was for the sleeping. Not enough room for three."

"But there was enough room for three when your brother came by, wasn't there?"

"Well, yeah, I didn't think about that."

"And since you weren't working that night . . ."

"Objection. It hasn't been established the witness wasn't working that night."

"Let's clear up that point. Were you working the night your brother arrived, the day before the search?"

"No."

"Well then, where did you sleep that night if your brother was on the couch?"

"In the double bed."

"With Petty Officer Lamm?"

"Well . . ."

"With Petty Officer Lamm?"

"Yeah, but we didn't do nothing."

"Thank you, Mister Kintner. No further questions."

"Can I go now?" Kintner gripped the arms of the chair, ready to sprint for the door.

"Very well, it's past 1600. This board stands in recess until tomorrow morning at 0900."

They filed into the passageway. Mark walked alongside Templeman. "Sorry your witness turned sour, Larry. I know how you must feel."

"It's not over yet, Markie boy."

"I'm sure it's not, Larry baby. Can't wait to see how you dress Lamm for tomorrow. Let's see, what's the most macho thing we can think of? Cowboy? Policeman — no, you used that one today. How about a football player? No pansies on the gridiron."

Templeman stopped, faced Mark. "Look, snipe, when I'm through with you and your bullshit charges you'll be lucky if Lamm doesn't charge you and your commanding officer with Article 138 for redress of wrongs. And it's not inconceivable he could sue you both in civil court for damages. It already happened once — remember the sailors who got tired of always being assigned lousy jobs? Didn't win but they gave their officers a wild ride. So hang onto your ass, Lieutenant, it may be the last you see of it."

Mark watched the lawyer walk away. The son of a bitch was right.

☆ Chapter Nineteen ☆

HE REMEMBERED the case Templeman had referred to, read about it in *Navy Times*. Five black sailors sued their officers for giving them nothing but the dirty work, they said. He had laughed along with everyone else at the idea of an enlisted man suing an officer on the basis of lousy assignments — or anything else for that matter.

He began walking toward the Spyder. Sure, he thought, they may have had unglamorous jobs, but every man has them sooner or later. Spent plenty of time myself scraping pots and cleaning heads. But I got out of it the same way everyone is expected to — work, advance. It built character, was the story.

The Navy once had strong support from the government, but since the Gulf War military people seemed to be taking it in the shorts from the Senate, the House, the President, the courts. Few in Congress had military experience. Sailors suing officers, cost-of-living pay capped every year — enlisted men's families on food stamps.

"Ah, hell," he said aloud as he reached the Fiat, "can't think of a thing to recommend the service, but I'm still here." His hand fell to the door handle and he paused. But *why* am I here? Why am I taking Bennett's craziness?

The career — always the career. It was the only answer he knew, but the sound of it was ringing hollow in his mind.

★

He pulled into the parking lot at the small bachelor officer quarters on Thirty-second Street. He needed a drink, and the BOQ club opened early. He started for the door, then remembered the briefcase on the seat. Better lock it in the trunk, he thought, walking back to the car. He lifted the case and his eyes focused on the building before him. Narrow white clapboards on the side reminded him of his lapstrake boat, built from plans and a kit he had bought through a magazine ad. He still remembered the name of the company. Rocky Cove Boats, Rocky Cove, Maine.

His mother had conceded if he earned his own money he could use the shed — a narrow, rickety clapboard garage full of the discards of years — to build his boat. Mark made the shed his own, setting up sawhorses he built from scrap lumber and fashioning a table against the wall to hold his plans.

He never finished the boat, but that didn't matter for what had fascinated him was the meticulous process of putting it together. In the shed, sitting next to the boat's bare framework, he had first read and dreamed about Alaska in John McPhee's book, *Coming Into the Country.* He imagined himself in the vivid descriptions — living off the land, trapping and hunting for food, sleeping in a cabin of his own construction or under the stars; fishing from his boat. In his mind, hiking in the shadow of Denali, he saw the bear McPhee saw, felt the wonder and the fear.

His mother never bothered him when he was with

the boat except to call him for meals, never showed any curiosity about it. He never asked her to see it. He left for the Navy with the lapstrake still in the tumbledown shed, narrow boards attached at one end that poked out from the curve of the side like shavings on a whittled stick.

He dropped the briefcase back on the seat and drove home to an apartment full of dead air.

☆

A frozen dinner heated in the microwave while Mark reviewed his notes. The television mumbled the news at his back. Sound. Without it, he felt as alone in the empty apartment as an ant in a soupcan. He shoved the legal pad aside and thumbed through the mail that had collected during his self-imposed exile to the ship. A few bills, ads for carpet cleaning, and a packet of grocery store coupons. Not even a magazine. Nothing from Lynn, but why should there be? Never had been.

The microwave dinner sat heavily. He opened a bottle of Maalox and sipped from it. The phone rang and he reached it in one step, quickly wiping his mouth and swallowing as he answered.

"Mark." Lynn's voice — the tone she used on phone solicitors. "I've been calling but just got your machine."

"I stayed on the ship for a few days working on that case. I told you I wouldn't call." Mark's guts churned in spite of the antacid and his palm sweated against the telephone receiver. "Will I see you again?"

"Saturday. Lunch at Bosco's. Noon." Lynn had issued the order.

The phone went dead. He stood holding the receiver, unwilling to release the tenuous connection it gave him to Lynn until the earpiece began to wail. He lowered it to the cradle and took his hand away. Little lines of perspiration remained on the plastic. Why face her? Call her back, cancel. No point prolonging the agony.

He reached for the phone, then stopped. Why keep banging my head against the wall when she can turn away from me like that?

"I don't need you, either! You're a liability to my social life," he shouted into the empty apartment. A dog began barking outside.

★

He wasn't entirely sure what, if anything, he liked about El Cajon Boulevard. For the most part the businesses along it had fallen into bleak storefront establishments, grimy coffee shops, used furniture stores. A few motels advertised X-rated video above their neon vacancy signs. Somehow the words *X-rated* and *vacancy* carried a different meaning when he saw them in juxtaposition. He had never liked explicit films, preferring the three-dimensional reality of making love. As he drove along the ridge that separated San Diego from the newer sections to the north, he concentrated on the exhaust note from the Fiat's tailpipe. It was almost May, still too chilly to have the top down in the evening, but he relished the cold slap of wind and the damp air. Like being at sea.

The small stucco house he faced had a red neon sign in the window, the only illumination in the tiny lot. ORIENTAL MASSAGE. He sat quietly for a moment. He knew what the sign meant in Asia. Not the same here. Probably no massage at all, he guessed. Probably on the off-limits list. Probably a big mistake.

"Another big mistake," he said aloud as he snatched the key from the ignition.

The building's interior was lit only by the backwash

of the neon sign and a small high-intensity lamp mounted on the wall, aimed at his face. A partition had been built across what had been the living room when the house held a family. Other than a small barred window covered with reflective material, the only break in the unpainted gypsum board was a peeling white door that looked transplanted from some other part of the house.

He pressed the SERVICE bell.

"Just a second, hon," came a muffled female voice from inside.

He waited, wondering what to do with his hands, settling on hooking them in his belt.

"What's your pleasure?" The voice was now behind the glass.

"Massage."

"You a cop?"

"No." His voice was flat. Probably looked like a cop, struck the same kind of caution a cop would.

The window slid up two inches and the voice came clearer. "Sorry, hon, gotta ask. It'll be seventy-five dollars up front. We'll talk more when you come inside."

He fumbled with his wallet and found four twenties. He slipped them under the glass.

The door lock clicked and he pushed through. A short blonde — mid-twenties he guessed — in a bikini held out a five-dollar bill. Her nails had been gnawed and were in need of a cleaning.

She padded down a hall lit with a single low-watt bulb hanging bare from a wire. Mark followed the blonde, noting the slight overlap of flesh at her bikini bottom. He still hadn't seen her face clearly, but admitted he had no real interest. What he needed was the touch of a female and he didn't much care whose.

The small room she directed him to was bare but for a red lamp and a foam rubber mattress on the floor. The mattress had a bamboo design on its plastic cover. That's the Oriental part, he thought.

He undressed. The shower was lukewarm. The towel was worn, smelled vaguely like bleach, and was too short to tuck around his waist. He held the towel at his hip with one hand and carried his pants with the other, dropping them both near the mattress.

The plastic cover crinkled as he lay face down and pulled the towel over his butt, a concession to modesty. *Tactile deprivation.* The term from a long-ago psychology class came back to him. He hadn't touched Lynn in more than two weeks. The ship was sterile of touch. Officers and sailors didn't touch. Except the gays, he thought, the irony making him smile.

"What's your name?"

He jerked, startled. He hadn't heard the blonde come in. "Ah . . . Mark."

"Okay, Mark, I'm Tracy." She knelt on the edge of the mattress and dragged her hands lightly across his shoulder blades. He chilled to her touch.

"Really tense, Mark. I won't hurt you."

"Don't mind if you do," he said, his words muffled against the plastic.

"Hey, I don't do that kinky stuff."

"No, I mean I like a hard massage, you know, *shiatsu,* like in the Orient."

"Oh," she said, "one of *those* guys. Well, I'll do what I can." She straddled his buttocks and ground her knuckles into his back. "Hundred, and I'll give you a ride you'll never forget."

"No thanks."

Barely ten minutes had passed when she slapped him on the rear. "That's it, seventy-five bucks' worth."

"Thank you, Tracy, it's just what I needed. You're very nice," he said, standing, letting the towel drop away, reaching for his skivvies.

She sat on the mattress, hair damp with perspiration. "What are you, anyway, one of them hard cases?"

"Just suffering from tactile deprivation," he said, pulling on his pants and socks.

"You're weird, mister."

He buttoned his shirt and let her remark whirl through his mind. "Yes, you may be right." Her world was simple, seventy-five for a phony massage, hundred more for a quick fuck. No analysis, no psychobabble. Cash on the barrelhead. The whore was nothing to him, but that was exactly what he wanted now. Nothing.

✯ Chapter Twenty ✯

The week's paperwork piled on his desk greeted him at 0600 next morning. A lot to do before reporting back to the hearing room at 0900. Casso had kept the paper work in priority stacks with small yellow stickies labeling each: HOT STUFF, PUT OFF, IGNORE. Good man, Mark thought. Better than me, spending the night trying to humiliate a whore, because I myself am a miserable shit.

He went through the first stack reading each word carefully and set one of the five letters aside because of a punctuation error. The endless reports surfaced next. What possible purpose could there be in a tub like *Modoc* submitting a Freedom of Information Act report on the number of outside requests for official information? There never were any. Nobody cared.

But the paperwork improved his mood. The familiar feel and smell of the buff folders were reassuring. The letters, all with the same structure, the same words, were like old friends now, dependable, reliable, something he could count on.

Dear Mr. and Mrs. [blank]

Your son, [fill in first name], has recently reported

> aboard USS *Modoc* under my command. I am pleased to have him aboard and I know this assignment will be an adventure and a maturing experience for him . . .

Nice gesture, he thought, even if it relied for its spontaneity on a twelve-page directive, complete with sample letters, from the Chief of Naval Personnel.

He finished the first half of the second pile by 0800.

The crew had assembled on deck for quarters. With any luck, the skipper would be there, too. Mark could leave the stack of folders in his cabin and head for Fleet Training Center and Templeman's bailiwick.

He tapped twice on Bennett's door, heard nothing and stepped in. The captain sat at his desk, a tray from the wardroom before him with a plate stacked high with bacon and eggs and a separate dish for toast. Mark noted it was about triple the normal ration. Bennett's mouth was full and he needed three swallows of coffee to clear it. He sucked for air, then dragged a napkin across his mouth. "Why aren't you at quarters, Mister Palmer?"

"Backed up paperwork. I'm on my way to the board. By the way, something Templeman hinted at got my attention — some talk of charging you under Article 138 for redress of wrongs and maybe a civil suit. You know, like the one in Seattle — the five sailors." Mark laid the folders on the desk and reached for the door handle.

"Wait a minute, mister." Bennett leaped to his feet, cascading bits of breakfast onto the desk. Pieces of egg spattered the folders.

"Actually, we were both threatened, Skipper, but I don't think he was serious. Just trying to rattle me, probably," Mark said, leaning on the back of a chair.

Bennett seemed to relax.

"But even if it happens, I don't think mine will stick. I'm operating under your written lawful orders, and this isn't Nuremberg or My Lai. Probably wouldn't get much press coverage at all. Unless, of course, the gay rights advocates were to get wind of it. Surprised they haven't already jumped on this one. But then, I can see Lamm's predicament. He says he isn't gay, so it would be a little embarrassing for him to be defended by them.

"But! And this is the interesting part, Skipper, when we — I mean the duly appointed board — find him to be gay, he's got nothing to lose by going to the papers, the gay rights activists, television."

Bennett slumped in the chair. "I think you're conning me."

"I'm just guessing at this point. Lamm's plenty pissed about this whole thing, this *kangaroo court,* to use his words." Mark moved to the desk and leaned forward on his hands toward the captain. "He's not queer, you know."

Bennett sat up, "I say he is, and goddamnit, I want him out. I haven't worked my ass off in this man's Navy to risk my future on a faggot."

"All right, sir, we should be done today. Then after I get the tapes and files off to Washington, it shouldn't be more than three or four months before we get authorization to discharge him. I guess you'll want to keep him in engineering, huh?"

"I don't want him on my ship. You understand that? I don't give a running fuck what that . . . that . . . bunch in Washington wants." Veins stood out on Bennett's neck but he carefully avoided criticizing the Commander in Chief — a violation of military law. His disdain, nevertheless, was clear.

"Sorry, Skipper, but it's right in the SECNAV instruction. We have to retain him on board." He watched the agitated officer throw himself back into the swivel chair, driving it into the corner of a file cabinet. "But look at it this way, *Modoc* is such a small ship we can keep an eye on him real easy." Mark grinned, enjoying the continuance of his trek along the narrow edge bordering insubordination.

Mark checked his watch: 0820. He clanged down the ladder, reaching the bottom as Frank Madera, the XO, stepped into the 0–1 passageway from his stateroom.

"Mark," he said, "glad I caught you. Let's have lunch."

"Now I *am* worried, XO. Last time you asked me to lunch I ended up chairman of the Combined Federal Campaign and Navy Relief Fund."

"Nothing like that. Let's just have a little lunch and talk."

"That's *really* serious. Look, I don't know when I'll be able to break for lunch with the admin board going on. Can we do it Monday?"

"Sure, Mark. No sweat. Good luck with the board."

Mark hurried to his stateroom and grabbed his briefcase. Must be mental fatigue, he thought. In my right mind I'd be more careful with Bennett and the XO. They must think I'm crazy — that I'm not taking them seriously. "Let 'em!" He mouthed the words soundlessly and headed for the quarterdeck.

★

Templeman appeared confident again in his sharply pressed uniform as he stood and walked around the table to the inside of the *U*. He did not sit on the table; rather, he propped his buttocks against the edge, avoiding any bend that might tug his shirt loose.

"Petty Officer Lamm, do you wish to make a statement to the board before I begin direct examination?"

"Yes, sir." Lamm looked at each member of the board in turn. "First I want to tell you all that I am not a homosexual and never have been. I didn't make sexual advances to anyone, least of all men in my own division. I believe some junior people wanted to get me off the ship and this is a way to do their dirty work. I have no animosity toward the board or Lieutenant Palmer. I think we are all victims of this charge, one way or another."

Penny looked at Will and Bert, then to Mark, finally back to Lamm. "Thank you for your statement. The board will consider it during deliberations. Counsel, please continue."

"Petty Officer Lamm, what specific reasons could there be for these people you speak of to want you off the ship?"

"Some men were using marijuana and I knew it. So I kept checking out the places on the ship where they might be sneaking a smoke. Almost caught some of them red-handed a couple of times but they threw the stuff overboard."

"Who were the men you suspected?"

"Overmiller, Arnold, Morris . . ."

"And Rambo?"

"Yes, sir, Rambo."

Templeman turned to the board. "You are familiar with two of these names, Overmiller and Rambo. One dead, one the unfortunate witness Lieutenant Palmer brought forward who told you a number of lies about Petty Officer Lamm. Petty Officer Morris was foolish enough to keep marijuana in his locker for Lieutenant Palmer to find during a health and comfort inspection. Next, Lieutenant Palmer found not only marijuana, but several hundred hits of LSD in Seaman Arnold's locker." He grinned at Mark. "That investigation cleared Petty Officer Lamm of any wrongdoing in the death of Fireman Overmiller." Back to Lamm. "Did Lieutenant Palmer interview you during his investigation of Overmiller's death?"

"Yes sir."

"And what did you tell him?"

"That some of the men had been smoking marijuana by the boat davits and it was possible Overmiller could have fallen overboard."

"And what did he say to that?"

"Something like it was the first sane thing he'd heard all day."

Templeman pushed off from the table and walked with measured steps to Mark's table where he replanted his hands and leaned forward, his face inches from Mark's. "Well, well, isn't that interesting?" He spoke to the board while looking into Mark's eyes. "Lieutenant Palmer concludes in his official report that Fireman Overmiller's death was probably the result of his own drug use and that Petty Officer Lamm was not at fault, in fact, was instrumental in clearing up the mystery."

"Objection." Mark called out.

"What is the basis of your objection, Lieutenant?" Penny asked.

"I'm not sure, sir."

A ripple of laughter went through the room.

"Well, can you tell me what you think it might be?"

Templeman shoved off and moved slowly back to his table.

"It's just that it sounds like an argument more than an examination. Unless Lieutenant Templeman came over here to examine the color of my eyes."

"I agree with that and I instruct you, Lieutenant Templeman, to stay on your own side."

Mark chuckled. Penny sounded like a father laying down the law to a pair of quarrelsome kids in the backseat.

"Yes, sir," Templeman said. "All right then, let's get on to the meat of the matter. Petty Officer Lamm, did you invite Fireman Overmiller to your apartment in National City for a welcome-aboard dinner?"

"Yes."

"And he stayed overnight?"

"Yes."

"Why did you invite him over?"

"Well, you said it, sir, a welcome-aboard dinner. Just that."

"Have you been giving these dinners long?"

"Since I reported aboard about two years ago. I gave a party for my whole division first so they could get to know me socially, then I'd give a dinner to the new men."

"Did you ever attempt a homosexual advance with any of these men?"

"No, sir."

"No further questions at this time."

Mark watched Templeman walk stiffly back to his chair, give his shirt a tuck at the back, and sit.

Now what? he wondered. Everything had been asked that made any difference. Templeman was a good lawyer, knew the territory. Even his apparent mistake — Kintner in his rent-a-cop uniform — hadn't seemed to hurt his case.

"Lieutenant Palmer, do you have questions for the witness?"

"Yes, sir, I do. Petty Officer Lamm, are you married?"

"Objection!" Templeman leaped to his feet. "I strenuously object. This question attempts to equate homosexuality with single men. Lieutenant Palmer has no evidence to give you so he relies on innuendo and stereotyping."

Mark felt cheap. Templeman was right in how the question would be perceived but he hadn't meant it that way. He didn't know how he *had* meant it, but Templeman had been waiting for it.

"I agree with counsel," Mark said, "it was a poor question and I withdraw it. Petty Officer Lamm . . ."

"Yes, sir?"

"Have you . . . ah . . . ever been approached by a homosexual? By that, I mean were you ever propositioned or accosted?"

"Objection."

"Yes, sir, if you count the benny boys in Olongapo City."

"By 'benny boys' you mean the street homosexuals in the Philippines?"

"Yes."

"And what was your usual response?"

"I never went with one of them, if that's what you mean."

"No, that's not why I'm asking. Please tell the board what you felt when these benny boys propositioned you."

"Sorry — I felt sorry." Lamm lowered his chin.

"That's an odd reaction. Explain." Mark had no idea where he was going.

"Well, I guess you know that most of the sailors would kick them around and call them names. I just felt sorry about that."

"So you had feelings for these homosexuals?"

"Objection. Lieutenant Palmer is putting words in my client's mouth."

Mark glanced at Templeman now sitting bolt upright, staring at him. Never ask a witness a question unless you knew the answer. The rule came to him from somewhere, probably an old television show, but it seemed valid.

"No further questions." Mark sat.

"Does counsel have any further witnesses to call?"

"Yes, sir," Templeman said, "I have one further witness."

"Very well."

"Counsel calls as its final witness Lieutenant Mark Palmer."

✮ CHAPTER TWENTY-ONE ✮

MARK DIALED the captain's number on the passageway telephone outside the hearing room, unsure what he would say.

"This is Captain Bennett speaking." His outside-line voice, like an airline pilot announcing thirty-five thousand feet and the Grand Canyon on the left.

"I've been called to the stand to testify."

"Lieutenant Palmer?"

"Right. Templeman has called me as a witness."

"Can he do that? He can't do that! Can he?"

"The senior member is checking it out now. We're in recess until he can review the instructions. Probably discretionary like most other points."

"What do you plan to do if he lets Templeman call you?"

"Under oath, what can I do but tell the truth?"

"Well, how bad could it be? You're the recorder, just object and don't answer."

"Objections aren't ruled on, just noted." A perverse enjoyment of the predicament that faced him and the captain invaded Mark's thoughts.

"What about the Fifth Amendment?"

"Doesn't apply in administrative proceedings. Besides, wouldn't it look a little fishy? Hell, it's almost funny."

"I don't see one goddamned thing funny about this. I'm going to have your ass, you screw me on this."

"Captain, you'll have to wait in line. I'll let you know how this soap opera turns out."

At the coffee mess, Mark dropped a quarter in the coffee can, and drew a cup of dark liquid. His mind was aroil. If his testimony was allowed, he sure as hell wouldn't lie for Bennett. How far is loyalty supposed to go? He had never felt the slightest tug of loyalty to Bennett personally, only to the position he held, he realized. But how is that split? If the man in the position has no respect, then by association the position has to suffer. Now Penny, there's an officer I can respect, but what chance do I ever have of getting to his position?

He knew the answer for Bennett. Fake it. Always worked before — tact — when he had the presence of mind to employ it. Make the skipper think you were part of the corps of ass-kissers and he'd leave you alone. Didn't matter much, anyway. In combat or emergencies you did what you had to do to keep the ship afloat, not out of devotion to the captain, but for survival. The rest of the time it was a job, just a job.

Hell, he thought, Templeman gets points either way it goes. A real feather if he should win. If he loses, it doesn't matter because chances were nil from the beginning and it is not a court case. At least, *he* can argue his true beliefs.

Inside, Mark self-consciously dragged his chair from the table and sat quietly apart from the group. To draw attention to himself, away from his lieutenant, Casso pushed his chair around roughly, slumped behind his tape recorder, and loudly cleared his throat, a protective gesture. Mark caught the petty officer's eye and grinned. Casso grinned back.

He wondered how Casso could keep all this in perspective. Lamm was his friend, Mark was his boss, and Casso was involved in the prosecution, even if only in a clerical capacity. I should ask one day how the personnelman could so calmly resolve the conflict in his own eyes. Might be able to learn something.

Penny broke the quiet. "I have studied all the available material during the recess, and the question of whether the recorder can be called as a witness is not addressed, nor do any of the general rules governing this procedure give even a hint at what is proper. Discretion and reasonableness are two terms used again and again in the instructions. Therefore, I'll hear arguments from both counsel and recorder on the subject. I will then make a ruling."

Sharp cookie, Mark thought.

"Since Lieutenant Templeman is the petitioner we will hear his argument first. Then Lieutenant Palmer may answer in rebuttal."

Mark watched Templeman shuffle through yellow sheets on his table, eye one briefly, then stand. "Thank you, sir. Lieutenant Palmer has been intimately involved in this case from the very beginning. He led the search team that went through my client's apartment, investigated the death of Fireman Overmiller, conducted a health and comfort inspection.

"Lieutenant Palmer has practically been a principal in this case. Now he is acting as prosecutor. Oh, sorry. *Prosecutor* is a term we can use only in judicial cases. But I'm sure you can understand my confusion since he approaches this case as if it were criminal. And indeed, should you find my client guilty . . . Again, forgive me for my confused use of terms, it isn't guilt you determine, only whether Petty Officer Lamm made homosexual advances. And of course, being an administrative body you don't sentence, you merely recommend what should be done with the accused should you find him . . . well, guilty.

"But think about this, gentlemen. For a man who has over twelve years' honorable service, and who has dedicated himself to the Navy, isn't a discharge *of any kind* punishment? Doesn't it mean he will be branded? Won't he be barred from work in companies with government contracts? Won't he lose his eligibility for retirement? Won't he be starting over from zero in the civilian world? Sure sounds like punishment to me.

"This is why I want Lieutenant Palmer on the stand before you. This board can be called anything, but it is a *de facto* trial court that hands down punishment just as any military judge or court-martial board might. That is the effect. The big difference here is that 'beyond a reasonable doubt' is a phrase foreign to these proceedings. My client is assured his rights will be upheld, but it amounts to little more than empty words when the basis for this whole gathering is a letter and a statement from a proven narcotics abuser. What rights are there for my client?

"Well, I'll tell you, gentlemen, what rights there are. The right to the whole story of why he is being held as the accused when any court, military or civilian, would throw this case out. There is no merit in the charges, so there must be another reason why Lieutenant Palmer pursues this case with such zeal. I want to know! My client wants to know! And, gentlemen of the board, don't you want to know?

"In his statement to you, Petty Officer Lamm asserted

we were all victims here. He included Lieutenant Palmer in that statement. Another victim. I believe he may be right. But are we all puppets dangling on somebody's string? I intend to find out.

"With his involvement in so many aspects of this case, the selection of Lieutenant Palmer to serve as recorder ranks with appointing Sacco to prosecute Vanzetti. I cannot see how he can present an impartial case for the government when he is *part* of the case. We owe it not only to Petty Officer Lamm but to our whole concept of justice and fair play to hear what Lieutenant Palmer has to say. I therefore ask the board to direct the recorder to take the witness chair."

"If you'll allow me a moment, sir." Mark scratched a few words on paper before his pen dried up, his thoughts with it. He closed his eyes and slowed the rise of his chest. In a few seconds a lightness came over him, clearing his mind, sharpening his focus on the words he would need to defend his position and himself.

Mark stood. "Gentlemen, I think you will find, should you care to check the tapes, that Lieutenant Templeman has treated this case as if I were a codefendant rather than recorder.

"Have I been involved in this case at another level? I would have to say yes. And I would say it because there is little option for anyone else to be involved. Overmiller's death occurred at sea and required immediate investigation. With a wardroom of eight officers, each with a function vital to the operation and safety of the ship, save myself, who would be the logical choice? Someone who hasn't experienced the rigors of sea duty," — he stared pointedly at Templeman — "and one who needs only lock his office door and go home at night may find this difficult to comprehend. But fleet units understand the importance of reasonable allocations of manpower and talent in a small ship at sea — a challenge that increases daily with downsizing.

"I am ship's legal officer, charged with handling inspections, searches, and investigations. But let me point out that my function is to protect the rights of those who are accused as well.

"Yes, I've been involved in the case because there was no one else to do it. And regardless of counsel's confusion over what he is before — a court-martial board or an administrative discharge board — he might do well to recognize that short of a court-martial, this proceeding is nearly all that's available to the sea service to handle problems that are too insignificant for the Navy legal system's time.

"But why should I testify? It seems a dangerous precedent to set. Am I bound to answer Lieutenant Templeman's every question regardless of confidences I have promised to keep, including those I hold as Classified Material Control Officer? And what kind of witness would I be? Certainly not an eyewitness. What about an expert witness? On what subject? A character witness?

"I would be forced to be a *hostile witness* since Lieutenant Templeman clearly wishes to discredit me personally."

He stood, fingers touching the tabletop, looking down at his notes. More would be overkill?

"Very well," Penny said, "I've heard two excellent arguments, both of which have merit and flaws alike. Since police are usually called to testify as observer witnesses in court, I am inclined to allow Lieutenant Palmer to be called, but his concerns are mine as well."

Will Tapia lowered his head and Bert studied the

ceiling, detaching themselves. Mark watched the three officers at the center table and suddenly realized Penny hadn't been influenced by Bennett's wishes. Will and Bert knew it, too. Penny would never have allowed Mark to testify if he'd had the least concern for *Modoc*'s captain. Mark glanced at Lamm, sitting, moving his fingers, knitting an invisible blanket.

Mark reached into his briefcase, found the oath card, stood with his right hand raised, and read the card aloud. He remembered the other oath he had taken almost ten years before; it wasn't much different:

> . . . that I will support and defend the Constitution of the United States against all enemies foreign and domestic, that I will bear true faith and allegiance to the same; that I take this obligation freely, without any mental reservation or purpose of evasion; and that I will well and faithfully discharge the duties of the office on which I am about to enter, so help me God.

He walked to the chair between the tables and sat stiffly, staring straight ahead like a new ensign at his first wardroom dinner. He heard the chair to his left scrape against the tile. He imagined Templeman standing, tucking in that goddamned shirt. Mark exhaled, slumped a little, and crossed one leg over the other.

Templeman cleared his throat.

"Want a cough drop, Larry?" Mark said quietly over his shoulder.

Templeman glared for an instant, then softened. "No thanks, Mark, this shouldn't take long."

In his unconcerned way, Templeman moved to Lamm's left side, closer to the board, facing Mark nearly directly. "Lieutenant Palmer, are you married?"

☆ Chapter Twenty-Two ☆

Penny's voice was totally lacking amusement. "What possible bearing on this case can Lieutenant Palmer's marital status have?"

"The same, sir, as the respondent's."

"I grant you that, Mister Templeman, but you'll remember the question was withdrawn voluntarily by the recorder when it didn't have to be. I want to know now if you plan to badger Lieutenant Palmer with personal questions."

"Sir, since I'm exploring motives here, it is necessary to understand the man first. So yes, I plan to ask additional questions that may be of a personal nature."

"Very well, but I warn you to remember you're speaking to a fellow officer whose dignity I refuse to let you impugn."

"Yes, sir." Templeman faced Mark again. "Well, *are* you married?"

Mark's heart pounded deep into his skull. He wasn't sure in this situation what his own rights were. If he didn't answer, was he in contempt of . . . board?

Bennett's puppets, Will and Bert, flanking Commander Penny, found it a good time to take notes and keep their eyes averted, mouths shut. Penny dragged a hand over his mouth and around his chin, stroking an invisible beard. He exhaled and shook his head slightly.

"Gentlemen, I see a problem here and I regret to say that I may have been the cause of it. We have no legitimate purpose in exploring Lieutenant Palmer's private affairs. Counsel will restrict questions to those relevant to the case."

Templeman grimaced, his expression verging on disgust. He turned to Lamm and shrugged, arms to the side, palms up, a quarterback looking to the sidelines after a blown play. Mark watched the little show, unsure what Templeman meant by the gesture. The lawyer turned back to him, held his gaze for a moment, sighed, and began.

"Are you acquainted with any homosexuals?"

"None that I know of."

"Let's say one of your friends admitted to you he was a homosexual. What would your reaction be?"

"Sir" — Mark glanced at Penny — "I object because the question is hypothetical. How could I know now what I'd do *should* the occasion arise." Mark leaned back, pleased with himself. Good answer, he thought.

"I agree," Penny said.

"All right." Templeman pressed his lips together and tapped his fingertips against his thumbs as if counting. A nervous gesture, not like anything Mark had seen him do before. He was too good at his work to get flustered. Had to be an act. But why?

"How long have you been in the Navy?"

"About sixteen years."

"That long? I would expect you'd be a commander by now."

"I have six years' enlisted service."

"Oh, then you understand what it's like to be enlisted?"

"I'd say so." Mark smiled slightly. Templeman had to be crazy to pursue this, he thought. Establish empathy between me and the enlisted men and he is defeating himself.

"You consider how the enlisted men feel about things when you give orders or establish policy?"

"Yes, I consider them, but I try to keep it in perspective. It may not change what I do, necessarily, but only how I might present the orders."

"That's very interesting and, I suppose, a noble approach. So you relate well to the enlisted men?"

What's he getting at? Mark questioned himself before answering, then, unable to prevent wariness from entering his tone, said, "I think I do."

"Then why do you suppose they refer to you aboard *Modoc* as Darth Vader?"

Mark laughed. "That's a new one on me. I've never heard that except from you, Lieutenant."

"Okay, then," Templeman went on not missing a beat. "Lieutenant Palmer, did you not yesterday have Fireman Rambo backed against a line of sinks in fear of his life?"

Mark twisted in the chair. He couldn't deny the last sentence. He'd wanted to hurt Rambo then.

"And did you know at this very moment, there are no fewer than six sailors aboard *Modoc* with chits for request mast, all waiting to talk to Captain Bennett — *complain* might be a better word — about Lieutenant Palmer."

The words came like a blow. How could Templeman have known? Beads of sweat trickled down the back of Mark's neck.

The lawyer stepped around Lamm, who now had his head lowered, resting on his fists, picked up a stack of papers and held them over his head. "I wish to enter these statements from the crew of *Modoc* as exhibits N through X." He placed a packet before each board member and handed one to Mark. "I admit I held them back intentionally because I had hoped I wouldn't have to use them to defend my client."

So that's what all the shrugging was about, Mark realized. Lamm didn't want the statements used.

"They refer to Lieutenant Palmer's actions aboard *Modoc,* and since they were about him and I had no way of knowing whether he'd be allowed to take the stand, it made no sense to give notification."

"That's bull!" Mark said, "Sir, you can't allow this character assassination."

"Kindly control yourself, Lieutenant. Now, we don't even know what's here," Penny said. "I think maybe we should read the statements, then hear arguments."

"But, Commander, if the board *reads* the statements you could be influenced by them, even if you don't allow them to be entered as evidence."

"Then how can I make a decision about something I know nothing about?"

"Don't allow the other board members to read their copies. If you choose to disallow it as evidence, then only you have seen it and you are still outvoted by the other members."

"That sounds reasonable." Penny reached for the copies of the statements before Will and Bert. The two officers appeared ready to protest, but kept silent. "Very well, I'll read these, and recorder, you read your copy. Everyone else keep quiet."

This is turning into a three-ring circus, Mark thought,

as he settled back in the witness chair to read the statements. They were mostly from junior enlisted men in engineering, the men whose lockers he had searched. He read without emotion the words that accused him of terrorizing the crew: *. . . even hear him yelling at lutenant Brown . . . everybody got questioned even if we didn't have nothing to do with it . . . acted like we was all criminals . . .* The English is abominable, he thought, as he finished the third. Eight more, probably all the same. He recognized the names, undoubtedly some of the same ones with chits in for request mast. Probably got a little friendly legal advice from Templeman about their right to complain to the captain. A little manufactured evidence.

His eyes slipped in and out of focus as he scanned the damning words. So what if they call me Darth Vader or Deputy Dawg, or anything they want? Who cares? It's my job and they can all go to hell. And not one word about the reason — did they forget Overmiller so soon? Their dead shipmate?

"Are you finished, Lieutenant?" Penny broke the silence.

"Yes sir, I am."

"I am ready to hear your objection."

"Sir? Sorry, sir, but you mean after reading this trash, you'll even consider allowing it?"

Templeman stood, grim faced, walked to the board table, gathered the packets, and walked to Mark. He reached for the statements and pulled at them. Mark held tightly for a moment, then slowly released the sheaf. Templeman stood so close Mark could smell his aftershave. The lawyer turned to the board.

"I withdraw exhibits N through X, and request a recess so I can shred this paper."

Mark was vaguely aware of chairs scraping against

the floor, of people filing out. He remained in the witness chair when they had all gone, head back, arms drooping at his sides. He stared at the acoustic tile ceiling, trying to make sense of random holes studded throughout the white. Getting used to being alone, he thought — practiced most of my life. Wetness left the corner of his eye and streaked toward his ear. He didn't bother with the handkerchief in his pocket. Alone in the room it didn't matter.

A single drop hit his collar.

"That's enough," he said, and reached for his handkerchief.

Outside, he walked between the platform-mounted ships' guns alongside the building. A crew in training on a Mark 45 Mod 3 five-incher lounged on the raised decking while a gunner's mate drilled them on procedure with rapid questions.

"Seaman Schwann, you have a hot gun and it's got a *hang fire* — you tried firing the round again but no bang — what are you gonna do?"

"Open the breech and unload the round?" the sailor on the spot answered tentatively.

"Schwann, you just got your bang — killed yourself and your crew. Now your commanding officer's gonna have to be writing letters to their mothers because *you* are not paying attention, Schwann! Anybody still alive — tell Seaman Schwann the answer."

"Cool the barrel inside and out with water so the round won't cook off," several men chorused, a single voice adding, "Dipshit!"

Mark listened a moment, thankful for something to carry his thoughts away from the admin board and his revulsion at himself. "Don't mess with Lieutenant Palmer," one enlisted man had written, "he'll have you for lunch." "I heard he was the one that pushed Overmiller overboard," said another of the statements.

Mark's face flamed. But what do I expect? Adoration from people whose lockers I searched, men I questioned? They probably don't even see the danger of Arnold running around the ship with LSD, only that one of their buddies had been nabbed by a "zero." "So whatsa matter with a little dope? It ain't even a crime no more off base, same as a parking ticket for pot. Fuckin' zeros, gotta be big men."

He'd heard it all before, no surprises, but on paper . . .

The gun crew moved to their places and began passing dummy shells awkwardly to the breechloader. Mark walked toward the quay, the sound of metal slapping metal diminishing. The sun was nearly overhead. He felt like hiding from it.

The past two weeks had been a disaster. Even allowing for his minor victory with Templeman's witness, Kintner, the presentation had gone badly. Am I naive, he wondered, or just stupid? What about that "special trust and confidence" we officers are supposed to engender? Haven't done too well with that one, not with the crew and not with the officers, either.

Reaching the concrete pier, he sat down on a bollard clean of gull droppings. He pulled his cap lower over his eyes, as if he could examine his life projected on the dark underside of the bill — instead of on a nest of destroyers snuggled hip to hip against a single pier. He remained, staring into the black nothingness of his cap's bill, lowering it like a final curtain.

☆ Chapter Twenty-Three ☆

THE HEARING ROOM looked the same as before the recess. Mark would present his opening argument first, then would come Templeman's closing argument, then his own closing argument. Simple. He had written most of what he would say. He had only to stand and read it to bring this charade to a close.

"Gentlemen of the board. Homosexuality is incompatible with military service. In this one sentence, the Secretary of the Navy stated the one possible policy that the Navy must cling to if it is to remain a strong, respected force."

Mark thought bitterly, sure.

"He further states that homosexual conduct seriously affects the ability of the Navy and the Marine Corps to maintain discipline, good order and morale and to prevent breaches of security."

Mark began to feel sweat gathering in his armpits, but he continued, "The basis for separation is simple: Petty Officer Lamm has violated the customary military superior/subordinate relationship by harassment of a junior member of ship's company."

He glanced around the room. Only Penny had his

head up, eyes focused on him. Bert Kastner had covered a sheet of lined paper with squares that he was now filling in a checkerboard pattern with his felt tip. Will Tapia's hands were together at the fingertips, his thumbs chasing one another in circles. Must have been watching Lamm. Templeman slouched sideways, absently taking notes.

Mark looked back at the pages he still had left and decided he could dispense with those that summarized testimony and evidence. What was the point? Now, he could feel his sweat staining his shirt. He flipped to the last three pages.

"Respondent's counsel would have you believe that most of the evidence presented here is not really evidence at all. That, of course, is for you to decide. I expect you will hear a theory about a conspiracy hatched by some drug-abusing sailors to get Petty Officer Lamm off the ship. We've been given no evidence of that."

"Clearly, Petty Officer Lamm has relinquished his ability to lead by violating the trust of his subordinates. And the weight of evidence rests squarely on his shoulders. Homosexuality is incompatible with military service, and so is Petty Officer Lamm's continued retention in the Navy." As Mark sat he felt trickles of sweat leave his armpits, making trails to his waist.

Templeman stood up, a confident face. "Gentlemen," he said, and they all looked up as though following a command. "There are some words in our language that carry heavy emotional impact. Just hearing them can cause us to react negatively. Such words might include *communist, nigger, whore,* and *homosexual. Queer. Fag.* Such words are so profound in their effect that when we hear them we begin to attach new meanings to otherwise neutral perceptions. That is what has happened here. This is a perfect example of how one word, *homosexual,* can significantly affect the thinking of ordinarily intelligent men. Here we have a variety of neutral occurrences. Two men share expenses as roommates, one invites another to his apartment for a welcome-aboard dinner, various uniforms are found in a closet. So what? Neutral. Meaningless, until they take on a new aura because of the effect of the word, the single word, *homosexual.* Now, significance flows like a Niagara of damning evidence because of our altered perceptions." Templeman's voice swelled to a crescendo.

"Here are some of the other so-called facts that gain stature only when the word *homosexual* is attached. Lieutenant Palmer attempted to point out the significance that Petty Officer Lamm is not married. You have my client's service record for review. The information is there. It means nothing whether he is married or not! But did you see Lieutenant Palmer squirm when the same question was put to him? He isn't married, either." Templeman faced the board holding his hands to the side, asking for mercy. What an actor, Mark thought.

But Templeman was not done. "Call a man a queer and he is then stuck with proving otherwise because guilt is assumed with the accusation. And where do we allow him to try to prove his innocence? Why, right here, gentlemen, right here! This is a simple, easy procedure. We needn't be concerned with rules of evidence or reasonable doubt, or even, and I mean no disrespect, a qualified judge. We can assemble a group of working officers eager to return to their work, and hold a friendly little meeting, hash this thing out.

"Well, gentlemen, that's *not* justice. It's not even good management. Take a murderer who was presumed innocent *in court* until proven guilty. He has a better chance.

Even if convicted. After serving time, becoming 'rehabilitated,' he can rejoin society. But if you hang a tag of *homosexual* on this man you have marked him for life. Homosexuals, whether real or the result of someone's overactive imagination, can't be rehabilitated. It isn't only God who makes homosexuals. A board of Navy officers can take a vote and create one.

"Of course you might be inclined to say, 'Where is the respondent's evidence?' But if we bother to think, it becomes clear that it is pretty tough to prove that a man is *not* what someone calls him. Finding evidence against these charges is like battling ghosts. So what can I offer the board?

"First, let me offer Chief Vega's testimony as to the value of my client to *Modoc* and the Navy. Now we can look at his service record. Twelve years of solid, honorable service, an evaluation average overall of 3.93 for all that time. Not bad on a scale of 4.0. He has medals for Desert Storm where he served honorably. How does that stack up against the word *homosexual*? Doesn't fit the preconception, does it?

"Not enough proof? Should I have rounded up some women to testify under oath to having sexual relationships with Petty Officer Lamm? Gentlemen, under these proceedings a man who has *never* had sexual intercourse with *anyone* would look guilty.

"I want you to think about the possible motives for this action against this fine petty officer and proven Navyman. Yes, he was the scourge of the drug users on his ship. How many of us take the time to do the same?"

Templeman's question struck Mark like an uppercut. If I *had* held routine health and comfort inspections, routed out the drugs, Overmiller might still be alive.

"Petty Officer Lamm said to you in his statement, under oath, that he believed we were all victims here," continued Templeman. "I think he's right, but only if we allow ourselves to be victims. That decision lies in your hands, gentlemen, for in your hearts you know that Petty Officer Lamm is innocent. Any other finding will truly victimize each of us."

Templeman took his chair. The silence lasted nearly a minute before Commander Penny turned to Mark. "Lieutenant, you have a final opportunity to present a closing argument."

Mark thought quickly about Templeman's argument. It had been a good one. Logical, coherent, with just enough emotion to avoid sterility. The truth — there's that, too. Mark's whole case had been innuendo and circumstance that he himself didn't believe. And he had handled his case, what there was of it, poorly. But then there wasn't a case to begin with. Bennett would be able to see that in the transcripts, even the summarized version. There seemed little point in a closing argument, but he dared not give the captain a reason to say he had quit.

"Thank you, sir." He remained in his chair. "If you will allow me a moment. . . ." He looked through his closing argument. He began crossing out whole paragraphs, circling only the sentences that seemed right. The others shifted uneasily in their chairs, while Mark sat quietly, turmoil raging inside him.

"Mister Palmer. Let us hear your argument." Penny's impatience and irritation became obvious. "What do you have to say?"

"Nothing, sir."

"Nothing?"

"That's right, sir, nothing."

Penny exhaled, exasperated. "Very well then, we will begin our deliberations."

★

After three hours of deliberation, the board reconvened. Mark wondered if he had been holding his breath the entire time. Penny looked haggard. Will and Bert sat quietly, heads down. The commander stood. "I regret we have not reached a decision. The board will meet again here Monday morning, 0800. Reporter, mark the time."

☆ Chapter Twenty-Four ☆

"HEY, BOY *san*. Up here."

Mark looked up, focusing on a silhouette jutting over the edge of the flat roof of an apartment building set down in the curve of the San Diego-Coronado Bay Bridge. The figure held a bottle in one hand and waved a flashlight with the other. "That yoou, Looouten-ant?"

"Hi, Tom."

"Come on up. Stairs around the corner."

Mark started up the concrete steps, unable to keep from laughing. Tom was an oasis, a place to go when life was raining grief. He had responded to Mark's call by inviting him for dinner, his voice carrying in its tone all the friendship Mark needed to know. He remembered the short conversation.

"Look, could we get together tonight?"

"Sure." Tom's voice had taken on a note of concern. "What's wrong? Is it Lynn?"

"Partly, but there's something else."

"I'll cook."

Mark suddenly realized as he pounded up Tom's stairs that the only time he ever saw his friend was when he had trouble. On the broad, flat roof Tom sat in a deck chair with his feet propped on the foot-high edge of wall. He poured a second glass of wine and held it at arm's length as if to entice Mark the rest of the way.

"Sorry, Tom." Mark took the glass. "It just struck me that when I'm in deep *kimchi* I track you down. That's gotta mean something."

"Cheaper than a shrink and I feed ya." Tom nudged the second chair with his elbow. Now a sigh. "I guess it is my fate to be father confessor to my flock of one."

A single bulb near the door illuminated the roof with harsh brilliance. The two men drank the wine and watched the indigo sky fight a losing battle with the glow of downtown San Diego. Harbor seals on a nearby buoy barked and a small fishing boat chugged near the shore. Mark talked until they surrendered to the chill of the night and with empty bottle and glasses walked down to Tom's apartment.

Tom basted his Bombay chicken and listened some more. He opened a bottle of Gewürztraminer and started his steamed rice.

The men sat close on the couch, Mark speaking in a tone normally used to propose a criminal undertaking.

"The one thing you haven't told me yet," Tom said, "is how you feel about homosexuality."

"What do you mean?"

"Well, what if, for instance, I told you I was gay?"

"Ha, now you sound like Templeman. He asked the same question."

"And?"

"And I objected that it was hypothetical."

"That's true, but why not be hypothetical for a minute? Crawl out of your military mind and try thinking without rules. Look, we all get in a box in the Navy.

That affects everything we do. Can't even go out and let her rip without worrying about the decorum expected of an officer. But back to the original question. What if I told you I was gay?"

"Are you?"

"You're dodging. Would you still come over here? Still want to talk, share a bottle?"

"I don't know what I should say."

"That's my point. The goddamned rulebook they issued along with your gold braid tells you what you *should* say, what you *should* think. How about listening to your guts for a change? Forget the *shoulds*. Talk to *me*!"

Mark shifted on the couch and took a sip of the wine. He approached the game as he would thin ice. "I guess I'd be intrigued."

"There you go. Curiosity. Might even be inclined to give it a try, right?"

"I didn't say that."

"Well think about this, then. What is the difference between you and Lamm?"

"Lamm got caught."

"That's what I mean. There is no difference. You don't believe he's guilty any more than you believe you're guilty, but he's stuck facing the charge."

"And I'm trying to nail him to the wall."

"Because Bennett told you to. How've you been sleeping?"

Mark lowered his head, the wineglass felt heavy in his hand. Blood coursed through his ears.

"I . . . I . . . keep thinking it ought to be me. Loner as a kid, lousy marriage . . ."

Mark felt Tom's hand on his shoulder, temporarily easing the emptiness that echoed in his chest.

"Got you thinking in spite of yourself. What if you weren't so gung ho? What if you weren't in the Navy, what would you be?"

Mark began to relax. He thought of his mother, his earliest memories, when she still held him, before he began insisting he was too big, too old to be cuddled. The girl in the massage parlor flashed into his mind, sitting there on the plastic mattress in her bikini, her words, "You're weird, mister." And his own reply. "Yes, you may be right."

A timer on the oven rattled in the silence of the small apartment.

"Hungry?"

"Starved," he said, but without conviction. "But what's the answer?"

Tom walked to the kitchen and started a spinach salad from ingredients waiting in a neat row on the counter.

"Whether I'm gay or not? See, it would add up for me like it would for you if someone wanted to build a case."

"Altered perceptions. What Templeman said in his argument. Neutral occurrences take on significance when we have perceptions altered by rumors and accusations. Conditioning."

"Smart man."

"Yes. He's a good lawyer, too. Don't know if it will be enough for Lamm, though. You know boards."

"Why don't you help?"

"How?"

"Can't answer that one for you. Come on, dinner's ready."

They ate in silence for a few minutes before Tom spoke. "So, how about you and Lynn?"

"Dead in the water. Calls me a liability."

"That's a gentle way of putting it."

"Meeting her for lunch tomorrow. Should prove to be interesting, if not downright disastrous." Mark took a bite of chicken. *Help Lamm,* Tom had said, but how?

★

Bosco's was the kind of place perfectly suited for a rendezvous. There were plenty of other unattached souls to choose from, even at twelve-fifteen on a Saturday afternoon. The seven-dollar brunch drew them in but the washtub-size margaritas kept them there long into the afternoon. A day at Bosco's generally turned out to be one in which you had no other plans, or if you did, they were soon forgotten.

Mark had asked the hostess to seat him at a table where he could see the door. She had wanted to put him back in the depths of Bosco's jungle, surround him with wicker, rattan, and an overgrowth of silk ficus and rubber plants. It turned out to be a lousy table, taking the full blast of sunlight reflected off the white walls of Bosco's bunker-like entrance every time the door opened. His mother could have walked through the door and he wouldn't have recognized her in the strong backlighting.

Mark had picked at a basket of chips since he had arrived, and now it was down to a few crumbs. The waitress had finally reduced her attentions to merely poking her head around the high back of the booth and raising her eyebrows. He tugged the corners of his mouth into an apologetic half-smile and slowly shook his head. He guessed she had him figured for a deadbeat. Eat the free chips, ogle the waitresses in their outdated tutus with the frilly panties underneath, and hope a dream girl would drop into his lap.

Twelve twenty-eight. He had given up watching the

door and pushed chunks of dripped salsa around the polyurethane tabletop with his finger.

"Sorry I'm late," Lynn said, slipping into the opposite seat. "Couldn't get away from Tony. Can you believe he brought slides of his last cruise and we had to sit there staring at Tony in Hong Kong, Tony in Africa, Tony in Singapore?"

"I don't suppose you could have told him to take a hike?"

"In front of Vicky?"

"Oh, never mind. Just a thought." He reached across the table for her hand and she reluctantly allowed him to hold it. "I suppose it's a rhetorical question, but how have you been?"

She lowered her eyes. "Tony wants me to come back."

"He's always wanted that. Why? Are you considering it? Of course you're considering it, otherwise you'd look me in the eye." He felt angry, yet somehow relieved. He watched her face as the bright shaft of light cast by the opening door lit her skin. Still as gorgeous as when they had met. She blinked and slid farther into the booth, closer to the shadowed corner.

"Don't do it."

"I didn't say I was." Her defenses were up.

"Want a margarita?"

"How about a table without a spotlight?"

The waitress led them back into the jungle. They remained silent while she brought their drinks and another basket of chips, and dropped a newspaper-style menu on the table.

"Whenever you're ready . . ." She left the sentence in midair and rushed to another customer waving at her from the darkness.

"Lynn," Mark began after half a minute, "I know these last few weeks have been rough and I haven't been much help. I found it hard to feel helpful when you wanted me to stay away. And it hurt like hell when you called me a liability."

"I didn't mean —"

"No, let me finish — even with my one-sided perception. I thought we loved each other. That meant a lot to me after Cora." He shifted in his seat. This speech was almost as difficult as the one before the board. "Since this thing came up with Tony, you haven't called me once, asked how *my* life is going, anything. Makes me wonder how much I *ever* meant to you." Was he pleading another case he didn't believe in?

"But you did. Do. And I thought you'd be okay. There's the Navy and your buddies. You have your work."

"You're really serious, aren't you?" He laughed at the irony. "Want to order?" He shoved the menu toward her and scanned for the waitress.

"I suppose I have been a little selfish, but you should understand the reasons. It's Vicky. I won't give her up."

"Have you talked to a lawyer?"

"What for?"

"What for! Tony threatens to take Vicky, get the custody changed, and you don't even see a lawyer. And you watch his slides like a good little Navy wife."

"It's none of your business," she whispered angrily, "and keep your voice down."

"It's my business that I spent two years falling in love with you, and you continually try to shut me off like a faucet. I feel like Vicky is practically my own kid. If it wasn't my business why would I lose sleep over it?" He raged inside as he stared into Lynn's face — how could she dismiss his feelings so handily?

"Ready to order?" The waitress appeared, her pencil poised.

The silence between them didn't lose its hard edge after they'd ordered. Mark's mind cast back on their two years, recognizing there had always been a vague feeling of dissatisfaction that had cloaked his time with Lynn. He wondered if it was real or just his mind protecting him from the inevitable. She had certainly always been willing to make love, but she hadn't once initiated it. *Tactile deprivation.*

Mark wondered how many more inane encounters were left in their relationship.

"How's Vicky been?"

"She has another loose tooth. Going to look like a jack-o'-lantern pretty soon."

"Here's to loose teeth," Mark said, lifting his margarita. She tapped hers to it, knocking a wet chunk of salt from the rim. It splattered the table. He put the margarita down. The time had come; there was no going back. "I still love you, Lynn, but I know now that we both need something different. Let's put this thing to rest. But I still hope you kick Tony's ass around the courtroom."

"Mark . . ." Tears left Lynn's soft blue eyes.

Mark felt stronger than he had in many months. He said, "Give Vicky a hug for me now and then. If she asks, I'm on a long cruise but I love her."

He shoved his plate aside. "Don't cry, Lynn," he said, "you'll make the chips soggy."

✯ Chapter Twenty-Five ✯

A mush of coastal fog had come in during the night and the Spyder objected in the only way it could, by refusing to start until Mark wiped the distributor cap with a tissue. He used another on his nose and swallowed a sinus pill from the pack he kept in the glove compartment. The four aspirin tablets hadn't started their magic yet.

Nothing helped. Maybe time was all that could. The booze and television only added pain in another spot behind his eyes. But the morning, even with the fog and an uncooperative car, seemed better than the endless hours since Saturday's lunch with Lynn. His notes had begun forming, taking shape last night, along with more margaritas. Now the handwritten sheets were in his briefcase on the seat beside him. He'd give them to Casso, first chance. He had called the OOD aboard *Modoc* to say that he was going directly to the hearing room. He had no desire to chance seeing Bennett, of being chewed out, cursed and threatened for his refusal to give closing remarks.

Have to change the wiper blades, he thought absently, as he peered through the fog-moistened windshield. Easier to think about little things than what had been prodding him during rational moments in the past few days — since Tom, since Lynn.

"Regulations. Orders. You just don't see the big picture. There are things you don't understand behind every decision." A response he had heard from the beginning. Used it himself once he advanced in rank. *Operational necessity.* How much it sounded like *in the interest of national security.*

He leaned back in his seat, straightened his thoughts into columns and read them off. On the basis of evidence was there enough to pursue Lamm? If not, was Bennett's order illegal? If it is illegal, then I am equally guilty of following it, or equally stupid? Where is the line drawn? Do illegal orders come in sizes? Felony, misdemeanor, infraction. Family size, economy size, giant size.

He worked his way through the traffic at the main gate and found a parking space near the Fleet Training Center building. On the barnlike main floor a crowd of sailors were talking, drinking machine coffee, and milling around the precommissioning check-in window. New crewmen for new ships. Plank owners. He recognized the nervous looks on the faces of the nonrated men, fresh out of boot camp, scared, confused. The old-timers wouldn't help with their sea stories of storms, fires, groundings. The ritual of intimidation and initiation into life at sea had already begun before a single new man had stepped aboard ship. Prey on ignorance, capitalize on fear, laugh while the new men learn to trust only themselves. Make them watch for the mail buoy or search for fifty feet of chow line.

He spotted Templeman leaning against the wall in the passageway outside the hearing room. The lawyer watched him walk toward the door, then held out a hand to block his way.

"You know it shouldn't have gone this far." Templeman's tone — somber, quiet — was a departure from his earlier cocky attitude.

Mark studied his face for a moment.

"Lamm is innocent and there's no point in denying it."

"No point," Mark agreed.

"What's Lamm supposed to do when they come back from deliberations and throw him out? Another four months of waiting around the ship, people pointing fingers at him, whispering, writing on the stinking walls, while the bureau makes the decision final. And the official review — probably some fucking junior civil servant with a rubber stamp." Templeman turned on his heel and walked toward the hearing room. Templeman thought Lamm was a goner.

Mark swallowed acid bile. He wanted to vomit, had to. He ran the few yards to the head and found a stall. His stomach emptied in a series of wracking spasms.

*

In the hearing room, Penny wore the same irritated look of last Friday afternoon. Will and Bert kept their heads down. "Reporter, mark the time. This administrative hearing board in the case of Machinist's Mate First Class Marion Arthur Lamm is reconvened."

Jim Casso checked his watch and marked the time sheet, busying himself with the tape machine, avoiding eye contact with Mark.

"Sir," Mark heard himself say, felt himself stand, "before the board continues deliberations I would like to say something."

"Arguments are closed, Lieutenant. You had your chance Friday and declined to take it."

"It's not an argument, just a statement, but I think the board should hear it."

While Penny barely nodded, Mark said, "If I had the authority, I would withdraw the charges against Petty Officer Lamm." He looked across the room at Lamm, who locked his eyes on Mark's.

Penny ran his hand over his stubbly hair and shook his head. "What authority are you calling on to even make such a remark?"

"A moral authority."

"Then why has this case gone this far? Why did you allow the board to reach this point? Why have you wasted the time of everyone here with your pursuit of this case?"

"Orders, sir."

"Then I assume you're still under orders. Aren't you in direct disobedience of those orders right now." It wasn't a question.

Mark sat down. There was nothing more to say.

"Lieutenant Palmer," Penny's voice badgered, "I ought to make a full report to your commanding officer concerning your statement here today, but I'm sure you'll do that for me." Mark scanned the room with a fitful, nervous eye, then glanced at his stack of notes. Only the movement of someone's chair broke the silence. Penny resumed, "If no one has anything else to say, this board stands in recess for deliberations. Reporter, mark the time."

They filed into the passageway.

"You dumb son of a bitch." Templeman stood close enough Mark could feel his breath. His voice continued low, a hiss. "What did you hope to accomplish with that piece of crap?"

"Had to say it, get it on record."

"If you wanted to help, you should have called me.

You got things real muddy now. You're not helping Lamm or yourself, especially yourself. You think you influenced them one bit?"

"They had to vote today, you know that."

"I also know that Lamm was a loss from the moment this whole circus started."

Mark stepped back a pace, hands to his side in supplication. "The review board in Washington — they're not stupid. They'll pay attention to a dissenting statement from a board member, right? What about from the recorder? If I buck the board on this, dissent on my own case, somebody might get the idea back there. This is a railroad and everyone knows it — here, Washington. Christ, I only want to give Lamm a last chance."

Templeman shook his head slowly. "Yeah, and you're going to have to jump the chain of command to do it! Mark, you fell on your sword in the worst possible way. And you didn't have to. Look, you only saw the statements I wanted you to, the ones that said you were an asshole. And I'm really sorry about that, but you didn't see the good ones — the ones that would have blown my argument to hell." He dragged his fingers through his hair, mussing it. "Shit, amateurs."

"I didn't know, but it's all right, you were doing your job. I understand that, Larry."

Now, Templeman's calm gave way to exasperation.

"There's something else you apparently *don't* understand. Why do you suppose the discharge rate is so high with these boards? Because most every sailor brought before one is guilty. Unauthorized absences, multiple captain's masts, drugs, fighting, general pains in the ass that cost more in administrative time than they're worth. With Lamm, there never was a chance once things got started. Just caught in the grinder — by mistake, by design.

Doesn't matter. Now you're jumping in after him." Templeman stalked away.

★

"This administrative discharge board has concluded its deliberations. By a vote of three to zero, the board finds that Machinist's Mate First Class Marion Arthur Lamm has attempted to commit homosexual harassment. By a vote of three to zero the board recommends that Machinist's Mate First Class Marion Arthur Lamm be discharged from the naval service by reason of homosexuality due to attempts to engage in homosexual acts and that the discharge be characterized as an *honorable* discharge."

Lamm's hands lay motionless on the table as Penny read the findings.

"Bailiff, reporter, and respondent are dismissed."

Chief Brown swung the door open and waited for Lamm and Casso to pass through before pulling it shut behind him.

"Gentlemen." Penny looked at each officer individually. "I am disappointed in this proceeding and in each of you. Some more than others. Lieutenant Templeman, you are right, I am not a qualified judge. But I am a qualified officer, and I, Mister Palmer, *am* following my orders to head this board.

"You will probably find out anyway from the other two board members, but I want this to be one thing you hear from me. I believe there has been a tremendous miscarriage of justice — if it can be called that — in this room. I'm not proud to have been part of it. I am not assuaged that to secure an honorable discharge for Petty Officer Lamm I had to bargain away my initial vote of not guilty to the charges."

The four other officers didn't move as Penny walked

out. Templeman finally kicked his chair back and left at a rapid clip. Then Will and Bert stood. Will stopped behind Mark.

"You fucker, Bennett's gonna have our asses over the honorable discharge."

Casso came in and began winding the microphone cords, gathering the stacks of paper still on the tables. "Sorry, boss. You tried. I think Lamm appreciates that, at least."

Mark looked up at the petty officer. "Well, it's not over yet."

Casso smiled. "Knew you'd say that. Knew it."

☆ Chapter Twenty-Six ☆

Frank Madera's jaw hung open, drooping, by the time Mark finished. "You dumb son of a bitch," he said, incredulous.

"That seems to be the unanimous opinion," Mark answered. "Just figure I'm crazy, okay? Will you give me a hand on this with the skipper? Just sit there in the corner and nod or look grim. Doesn't matter as long as you go with me."

"I've told you over and over about this. You're not going to change anything." Frank's voice went calm. "You know it's a game of perceptions; that's why admirals are square-jawed, beetle-browed, heroic-looking types. Bennett has to hang tough any way he can because being a little bit soft — or soft-looking — can jeopardize a promotion."

"You going to help?"

"To get the skipper to drop the charges? You *must* be crazy." He leaned forward. "Remember we were supposed to have lunch together today?"

Mark vaguely remembered agreeing to Monday lunch.

"That wasn't supposed to be a social occasion. Skipper's been on my case . . . I'm supposed to counsel you."

"Can all that wait?"

"If I'm going to kick your ass, *I* get to set the time!" Frank tapped his pencil on the desk blotter. "And that seems to be your whole problem. You think you run the goddamned ship — maybe the whole Navy. And it's only been since you reported aboard *Modoc,* according to your records. You act like nothing here is good enough for you."

"Excuse me, Frank." Mark hoped he appeared dignified. "Please spare me the official indignation; your heart's not in it and you're doing a terrible job. *Will* you help me with Bennett?"

Frank looked abashed and slightly nervous. "You got a hell of a way of asking. You come in here, insult me, then expect me to help you?"

"Not me. Lamm. Frank, haven't you been listening? He's innocent. No question about it. Help *him.* Bennett won't listen to me alone — not about this. That's why he sics you on me."

"It's the chain of command, Mark. Ever hear of it?"

"That's why I'm here now, instead of beating on Bennett's desk."

"So you want me to sit there while you commit suicide. Once the captain comes down off the overhead, he's going to ask what I think, if I talked to you before letting you bring this beef to him." Frank's jaw twitched. "One thing I'm telling you right now, nothing's going to get in the way of my retirement — like testifying at your court-martial. I'll let you in on the truth." The XO shook his fist at Mark. "I think the best thing that could happen is what did happen. Lamm is getting an *honorable* discharge. Bennett can't downgrade what the board recommends, right? So he's stuck with that as the worst."

"What about Lamm's twelve years and 4.0 marks? Doesn't that count?" Mark resisted the urge to put *his* fist in the XO's face.

"That's probably what got him the honorable."

"He's innocent."

"Okay, so he's innocent!" Frank's face was changing from russet to scarlet. "What difference does it make? Every sailor on this ship thinks he's guilty. What chance would he have in a leadership position now? Once a man is held up for ridicule, right or wrong, he doesn't have a chance of being taken seriously. Overmiller calls him a queer and he's a queer."

"Not quite, XO. Overmiller had help."

"The conspiracy, huh? Arnold? Rambo?"

"No. Bennett, me, you. That conspiracy." Mark spoke carefully as if to a small child. "If we had done what we should have done with that piece of trash Overmiller wrote — shitcanned it — that's where it would have stopped. Maybe if Bennett drops the charges now, I could arrange for a quick transfer. Get Lamm on another ship, give him a chance to start over."

"Navy's too small for anyone to outrun a thing like this. No, it's better if he's discharged." Frank was dismissive.

"And that's it, Frank? Just write him off without a chance? Why not ask Lamm what he wants? Aren't we short of engineers? Doesn't anyone care what Lamm wants?"

"Stay the hell away from Lamm." Frank's voice began to tremble. "You don't take a board's recommendation and let the respondent pass judgment. That's not only insanity; it shoots holes in the whole system. Let Lamm appeal if he doesn't like it."

"Frank, there *is* no appeal. He's stuck with what the board does unless Bennett throws it out."

Frank laughed scornfully. "You can forget that. When did you ever see the skipper make a reversal on anything? He's always right, or always the captain — means the same. He sees changing his mind an admission of failure, inadequacy of his original thought. Haven't you figured that out?"

Mark tossed his head back and closed his eyes. When he opened them, the white-painted overhead, criss-crossed with pipes and wire runs, was out of focus.

"Frank," he said, willing his eyes to shape up, "with or without your permission I'm going to see Bennett."

Frank leapt to his feet, shoving his chair violently against his desk. "You're really pushing your luck."

"Aye aye, sir!" Mark stood. "I guess this means I'm on my own." He took two paces to the cabin door. "Guess I've *been* on my own all along. And if this qualifies as counseling, we can skip lunch."

"Mark, don't fuck yourself this way. Is Lamm worth it?"

"*He* is. Don't know if any of the rest of us are."

Mark pulled the door closed. The passageway smelled of paint, and a pair of sailors stubbed their cigarettes when they saw him.

"Porter, Benbow, get some hatches open, then go up on deck for a couple minutes. Take a break, you need the air. And the smoking lamp is out while you're painting, no need taking chances, right?"

"Right, sir," they chimed together, then scurried away.

Dumb shits. What's the Navy coming to?

☆

The first thing the captain said, without preamble, was "Mark, what's the verdict?"

"Recommendation for honorable discharge."

"Honorable. Honorable? That's not what I —"

"Ordered? Is that the word, Captain? You told Will and Bert to nail him regardless of the facts. You wanted insurance. But there wasn't any evidence. Lamm is innocent. I told you that before."

"But you won the case, Mark. The insurance was for you, too. You'll be a lieutenant commander in a year. Think about those gold oak leaves."

"Why did you force me to go through this? You really believed from the start that Lamm was guilty?"

"Well, at first, of course, there seemed to be sufficient evidence to warrant action against him — but you needed this, too. Quite frankly, I was beginning to wonder about your loyalty, and this case was a perfect opportunity to display . . ."

"Why don't you admit you made a mistake and wouldn't reverse yourself even when you knew Lamm had done nothing?" How much more of this can I take before I go berserk, Mark wondered.

"How can you be so sure Lamm hasn't done anything?" Bennett protested.

Mark took a deep breath. He was reminded of his farewell to Lynn. "Look, Skipper, this thing has been a big strain on everyone, you included. I know that. I know what SECNAV says, too, but there's something more here. Drop the charges and you'll be a hero. You don't believe Lamm is guilty any more than I do, so what do you have to lose by letting me quash the whole thing? It would be the humane thing to do. The man's had enough."

Templeman's words came back to Mark — *you'll have to jump the chain of command to pull it off . . . you fell on your sword . . .*

Bennett finally spoke. "So what do you want?"

"Throw out the board's recommendation, burn the so-called evidence. I'll call the bureau and see if I can arrange a quick transfer for Lamm. That way nobody loses. The Navy keeps a good petty officer and engineer and you're rid of him. In spite of all this, Lamm is still a good sailor — why, I don't know. Give him this chance, Skipper."

Bennett got up from the desk and walked to the chessboard. He picked up a knight. "You're still forgetting that I have you dead to rights as a liar. Who's going to believe anything you say when I court-martial you?" He smiled.

"I'll be sure my lawyer gets that part in context. 'Lieutenant Palmer, did you ever lie to Captain Bennett?' 'Yes sir, once. He wanted me to play chess and I didn't want to play. I said I didn't know the game.' And I know just the lawyer to defend me." Mark laughed derisively. "Let's go to court, Captain. I have nothing to hide. How about you?"

He could no longer ignore the rage that was boiling over. Bennett had destroyed Lamm simply because he could. He had perverted the honored power of command — of an officer's duty to take care of his men.

Bennett reached down to the chessboard and fingered a pawn. "Mark, you need a break from all this. You can have a bright future — think about what you're doing. Look, I'll make you chief engineer. You and Dave can switch jobs. You're senior, anyway."

"Drop the charges against Lamm! Kill the case!" Mark heard himself ordering.

"I can't do that."

"You mean *won't*."

"All right, *won't* then!"

"Let me guess. You'd sell your mother for another gold stripe. It's easier to sacrifice Lamm than to admit you overreacted. You can't allow even a hint you're soft on homosexuals. How would *that* look to a promotion board!"

"You insubordinate shit." Bennett took a step forward, fists clenched.

Mark stepped back a pace. He had hoped it wouldn't come to this. He unbuttoned a single button on his shirt — just above his belt — and reached inside for two envelopes he had placed there earlier. He drew them out while Bennett watched, curiously, now silent.

"I had Casso type these up for me." Mark held up the thicker envelope. "This one describes the Lamm case and how you ordered me to pursue it even when I told you I had no evidence, even when I told you everything pointed to Lamm's innocence. It also states how you ordered Will and Bert to vote on the board. There's a whole lot more in here."

"I order you to give me that letter," Bennett said and lunged forward. Mark danced to the side. Bennett crashed into his game table, sending the onyx board and chessmen scattering against the bulkhead.

"Oh, you'll be provided a copy. This one is for SURFPAC."

Bennett drew himself up against the wall, rubbing his elbow. "You just ruined your career, mister. No officer scuttles his CO without going down, too."

"Thought you'd say that, so I brought a letter you *can* have. My resignation." Mark laid the second letter on the ruined chessboard. He opened the cabin door, took one final look at Bennett's tortured face to burn it into his memory. He tucked the thick envelope securely under his arm and pulled his garrison cap from his belt. On the main deck, he stepped to the brow and faced aft. *Modoc*'s ensign fluttered on the jackstaff. He brought his hand to his eyebrow in a stiff salute and held it. As he dropped his arm and walked across the gangway to shore, he could feel his heart beating a quick tattoo.

★

Nothing good happens fast in the Navy, Mark thought, as he guided the orange Spyder down Harbor Drive. For that matter, most of the bad things take forever.

But for the first time in months, he felt that somewhere in the mess he had created at the discharge board, he had found within himself a nugget of character. And he liked the feeling.

His slow progress up Harbor Drive past the shipyard at National Steel and Shipbuilding took him near the tuna cannery and he sucked a deep breath of the hot smell of cooking fish, realizing he didn't really dislike it. Everyone else did, to hear them talk, and he had complained too — because *they* did. He glimpsed that lifelong paradox in himself, that willingness to go with the crowd over something as clear-cut as the smell of fish, but stiff as iron the rest of the time — when his dissent might have mattered.

Past Seaport Village he drove, caught sight of the Harbor House Restaurant and thought of Tom LaCroix. "Forget the *shoulds*," Tom had said, "listen to your guts."

He parked near the Broadway Pier and snugged his garrison cap against the breeze coming off the bay. He felt like a tourist in his own city — not necessarily a stranger, but curious. Small things stood out that he'd never noticed before — the hot dog stand near the harbor cruise dock, the unused trolley rails. How many times had he stood on the pier next to the *Star of India,* without going aboard?

He walked toward the boats tied further down the quay. Seiners — the huge fishing boats that belonged to the San Diego fishing fleet — bumped against their fenders. The larger boats carried tiny helicopters tied to landing pads atop the wheelhouses — dragonflies stopping by for lunch. The wide-flared bows and low sterns made the ships appear to be moving forward even while tied securely to the pier. He stopped at a blue and white seiner, the *Mandy Beth.* Mark watched a man in tar-stained overalls pick at a huge pile of nets, inspecting each knot. He was in his twenties and sang softly to himself as he worked.

He checked his watch. Sixteen-thirty . . . no, four-thirty. "Four-thirty, Post Meridian," he repeated aloud. "*Civ-ill-yun* time," he said. "*Civ-ill-yun* time, *civ-ill-yun* life."

Back in the Spyder, Mark looked in the mirror. He straightened to attention in the seat and flipped one collar point up, revealing the clasps that held his lieutenant bars. He took them off and dropped them on the floor. Then the other bars came off, and his ribbons and name tag.

"*Civ-ill-yun* clothes. *Civ-ill-yun* body," he said and flopped back in the seat. Lacing his fingers behind his head, Mark stared at the water, making images in his mind of the wooden lapstrake boat he had never finished building.

"Gonna build that boat," he said aloud.